WeaponiZed:

They Sent Their Failed Experiments to Destroy Us.

Written and Created by:
MICHAEL E. ESSER

This is for my daughters Addison and Alexis.

I love you and your legacy is my motivation.

To my daughter Jeanina, your sudden passing away has not only been the most horrific thing I have ever had to deal with, but the loss has been one of the most powerfully painful lessons I've learned.

Life is short.

Love unconditionally and live right for today, because tomorrow you may only be a memory.

PART ONE

THE INVAZION

The sound of sea water sloshing between the docks and the ship's hull is interrupted by the grinding of a large crane that's off-loading oversized metal shipping freights on to the dock.

The whine of the metal stressing as it grasps its latest haul is suddenly followed by the snapping and clank of an oversize bolt as it hits the concrete below.

The crate in its grasp swings uncontrollably as it violently smashes against its neighboring crates. The impact of the collision peels back a small gap between the iron doors and the containers thick wall.

Without warning a large man with spiked hair, gray skin, and yellowing eyes peeks out through the opening. As he begins to pull himself up and out of the container, it's revealed that he has no lips and his tattered hospital scrubs are smeared with blood.

He hits the ground and looks around as if he is sniffing the air. His motions are so slow and methodical. Then, just as he turns to escape down the dock, he growls at the night.

In the skyline, two marksmen were already positioned and watching over the unloading of the crates. With each shooter on different rooftop, they waste no time firing at the escapee.

The first shot tears clean through the targets leg and bounces off the ground and ricochets off a metal container in the near distance. A second one tears through its shoulder and dings off a nearby container, but the beast isn't fazed.

Finally, both marksmen decide to aim at the head of the beast and releases shots at the same time hitting its mark with such velocity the entire head is disintegrated from the dead man's shoulders. The beast drops to its knees and slumping over lifeless.

"Make sure we seal the area off." One of the gun man mumbles in a Russian accent into a microphone attached to an earpiece, "It's not time to release these damn things."

The other shooter nods and leads a group of workers down to attend to the damages.

Without wasting any more time the crane winds back up to resume off-loading what looks like an infinite number of remaining containers as the sound of activity again consuming the air.

CHAPTER ONE

HONOLULU, HAWAII
ONE YEAR EARLIER

An elderly scientist stands in the morgue of an old army hospital.

At first impression, he look's completely mad and his eyes are filled with what can only be described as crazed-exhaustion. His sleeves are pulled up to his elbow, revealing two wrinkled and time-worn swastika tattoos.

He begins to grumble under his breath in a sadistic, heavy German accent as he stands hovering over a very ill looking elderly man who he callously jams his finger into his chest and side as he rambles off a laundry list of diseases that riddle the man's body.

The room, full of hand selected international scientists and military commanders, stands speechless.

"What I've been working on for the last 62 years is a cure for all of these things and more. I believe I am close to accomplishing my goal through both chemical and cellular therapy." He places an oxygen-style mask over the ill man's face and begins to administer a dose of an unidentified gas.

Within seconds, and like a miracle, the sick man's color instantly returns to his face and his gray hair begins filling in a natural dark brown color. His wrinkles disappear and his skin becomes tighter as the bright blue color returns to his half opened eyes. It's as if someone has turned up the light on a dimmer switch.

His once flabby, bed ridden muscles fill out and inflate as if they are being pumped up and quickly double in size.

"Uhh-huh," the clearing of the man's throat startles even the most hardened military man in the room and he attempts to sit up for the first time in years.

The doctor approaches with his hands clutched together "Now let us test his blood and go through the results together."

Just as the final vial of blood is drawn, and with no warning, the man collapses back down into a slump. His body wastes no time regressing, as he rapidly returns to its original state, and then gets worse. He begins to contort and twist until death passes him and what's left is a creature that can no longer be considered alive. It's like something out of a horror flick. Puss and ooze begins to creep from the corner of his eyes and his mouth. The doctor pulls a revolver from his lab coat pocket and shoots into the beast's temple.

It ceases its movements.

Again leaning over the decayed body, the elderly doctor reveals his goal for the demonstration.

"I want each nation to take this data and chemical samples of my life's work. I want you to work towards a solution that we can all share."

As this is being said, there is no sense of camaraderie in the crowd. This has quickly become more like a race to control the miracle drug, than it is to share in anything positive.

KAZAN, RUSSIA
THREE MONTHS LATER

In the research ward of the local government ran hospital, a familiar overweight orderly with spiked hair is changing the trash liner in the hazardous waste basket of a sleeping patient's room.

His earphones are pumping music at such a volume that his mind is elsewhere.

In the background, the once catatonic patient who remained motionless for months is now slowly rising. Her bare pale feet take step after step towards the unsuspecting attendant. A single beam of light creeping through the door hits her face and reveals her yellowed eyes and recently self-chewed off lips.

Replacing the bag in the receptacle, the orderly turns and is startled, just as she lunges at him teeth first.

SIX WEEKS LATER
BEIJING, CHINA

Two young scientists wearing clean, white lab coats argue back and forth in a heavy Chinese dialect as they are standing on the lighted side of a doorway leading into a very dark room.

As the conversation becomes more and more heated, one of the men begins to repeatedly slam his finger into a stack of medical charts he's holding, while the other continues his rant while hectically pointing into the dark room.

A strange noise from the darkness causes the two men to pause momentarily in silence. But they quickly resume their debate.

A moment later, another, louder series of bangs and moans start to come from the blackness in the room. Curious, one of the men reaches into the room to flip on the light switch. He's instantly yanked into the dark without warning.

There's silence and then suddenly the man howls in pain from the darkness. At first frozen with fear, his screams cause the cowardly man to attempt to turn and run. He doesn't take a single step before he's pulled back into the room from behind. The speed and force is so fierce it lifts him off his feet.

Just as the erratic flashes of the old neon lights begin to flicker, the chaotic, blood soaked room reveals the half a dozen empty beds that were once occupied by the blurry beasts now devouring the two overseers.

CHAPTER TWO

KINGMAN, ARIZONA
PRESENT DAY

The sun is creeping up over the cold desert mountains as the sunlight slowly fills the bowl that is the Kingman Valley. The landscapes still silent until the sudden rush of a wild jack rabbit bursts through the dried brush.

Immediately on his tail pounces Al, a large, determined German Sheppard and gray wolf mixed breed mutt. The chase continues over the train tracks that line the length of the town, across the famous Route 66 highway, and through a hole in the chain link fence that surrounds a blue, single-story house with large trees that seem to shade the entire yard.

Up and down the old dirt road all of the light poles are littered with campaign posters and yards are dotted with campaign signs that all read, "Smith for President."

Inside the home, Dr. Jason Martin, an athletic looking Hispanic man, is sitting stretched out face down sleeping at his chaotic desk. The wall behind him is full of degrees and awards. Amongst the mess there's a microscope and some other scientific equipment.

Without warning, the screech of his morning alarm startles him to his feet. In a panic and confused he doesn't even notice the post-it note that's stuck to his cheek.

Into the room walks his oldest niece Alexis, a cute 17 year old girl with dirty blonde hair and an obvious sense of fashion. She has a cup of coffee in one hand and a tablet reader with the local morning newspaper displayed in another. She stops to silence the alarm before setting both down on the clearest possible spot on the desk.

"Uncle Jason?" She says acting obvious in the fact that she wants something.

"Yeah?" Jason replies plopping back down into his chair sensing her motives and finally noticing and removing the post-it from his cheek. "What would you like me to say 'no' to today?" He asks sipping the coffee.

"Well, I'm not sure if my dad will be home in time tonight to ask, but I've been invited to a movie tonight with my friends and I was hoping it'd be alright if I go?"

Jason snickers and shakes his head.

"Are you serious? You just got into trouble with that Sam character and we all agreed that if you wanted your freedom back we needed to see some serious effort on your part."

"I know, I'm trying, but if I don't say yes he'll ask Jenny Sheets and forget about me."

"Sam Green is a punk who is on probation and court ordered to takes drug tests because of a drug possession. You can do better, so it's out of the question for tonight." He says pausing for a moment to flip through the digital newspaper on the tablet before returning to the conversation, "Anyway, you've got to watch your sister until either your dad and aunt get home, just in case I run late again."

"You're always running late," she says irritated before sarcastically adding, "The absent minded chemist who's consumed by his work."

"I know it sucks, right?" he adds mocking her tone and matching her sarcasm.

She huffs and turns to leave the room with attitude.

"Make sure your sisters getting ready!" he yells out after her.

Meanwhile, Addy, Alexis' younger sister, is standing in the front doorway holding a bowl full of dog food, calling out, "Al! Breakfast time! Come and get it! Come on boy!"

Alexis steps out from behind the door, "Leave that crazy mutt out there and go get ready for school."

Just then, Al returns with his prize, the dead rabbit in his mouth. Addy bends over to set his bowl down and tugs on the rabbit's tail.

"What's this? You get your own breakfast?" Addy asks Al in a little puppy dog voice.

"If I knew that dog was going to be such a good hunter, I might have actually taken up the sport." Jason adds from back in the kitchen where he smells a shirt that he's picked up off the back of the couch. "Hey, you know whose coming home today?" He continues.

"Daddy!" Addy say bubbly as she shuts the door.

"Yep, Aunt Cindy went to pick him up from the airport in Las Vegas." Alexis adds.

"I wonder how long it takes to fly here from Korea." Addy asks.

"I'd say at least a half a day or so." Alexis answers, "You can ask him when he gets here later tonight."

LAS VEGAS, NEVADA
MCCARRAN INTERNATIONAL AIRPORT

The large electric board that tracks flights switches from "On Time" to "Arrived" next to the flight from Los Angeles to Las Vegas.

Cindy, in her mid-twenties with dark hair and a sort of 50's rockabilly style about her waits patiently chewing on her thumbnail.

An elder man with a flashy fashion sense stands a few feet away looking more eager as she is. "I'd wish they'd let us back to the gates like they used to before all this 'threat of terrorism' crap took over." He comments out loud to no one in particular.

"Yeah, this waiting is killing me too." Cindy adds.

"Boyfriend?" the man asks plainly.

"No, I'm just waiting for my brother, how about you?" She asks back to be polite.

"My boyfriend." He replies.

A little stunned at his answer, she deviously smiles back at him and the two exchanges a mini high five.

"Mine's been on business in Japan for six months and I don't care what you say, video chatting on Skype is not enough." The man adds.

"I know, my brother Mike left last year for his last deployment in the Army and it feels like he's been gone so long. He has two beautiful daughters waiting for him at home."

The automatic doors open and a clean cut large man, in his mid-thirties with dirty blonde hair walks through dressed in Army fatigues and carrying a military green shoulder bag.

He smiles ear-to-ear when he sees Cindy. The two hug and he lifts her off her feet. As Michael sets her down, she turns to see the elderly gentleman hugging his younger boyfriend and she gives him a wink and he replies with thumbs up.

After a moment, everyone begins to migrate towards the parking lot, dragging their luggage behind them.

"So, do you want to stop and get something to eat here or do you just want to head straight back to Kingman?" Cindy asks as Michael throws his bags into the bed of his old black pickup truck.

"I don't know. I've been living in what feels like an ant farm for a year and Vegas really seems to be no better. I mean look at all these people." He answers looking out over the ledge of the seven story garage structure, "I mean, if something were to happen here, this place is like an island. He adds digressing, "It's cut off from any major area for hundreds of miles, not to mention the mountain terrain. Its only defense is Nellis Air Force base and those fly boys are only good for wiping a place clean."

Cindy begins to snap her fingers with sass.

"Alright 'army-man' I want my brother back."

"Sorry sis," he turns and opens the truck door, "I say we get back home to the quiet, peacefulness of small town living as soon as possible."

"Good." She says as they exchange a look.

They climb into in the truck and pull out and down the corkscrew shaped exit ramp and wait their turn to merge with the massive amount of traffic that stretches for miles to the Las Vegas Strip.

CHAPTER THREE

KINGMAN, ARIZONA
TECHNICAL SERVICES LABORATORY

Jason is alone in his lab, looking down into a microscope. He's examining samples of a solution that he's extracting from multiple glass tubes.

He's speaking into a recording device.

"Upon further tests of the Air Forces so called 'Solution X' I feel that the problem with this anonymous project isn't entirely about the chemical makeup. I feel what's wrong with the original formula is that it is a combination of things. Basically, it's missing an important protein and in need of a massive adjustment to the concentration of the final solution."

He adds a drop of blood and a drop of his solution to a slide and examines it further under the microscope. The solution incorporates with the cells without causing any adverse reactions. He turns around and sets up two syringes of his mix and prepares to pulls two rabbits from their cages by lifting off each cages cover.

One cage is labeled "infected-cancer" and the other is labeled "controlled-clean".

He opens up and reaches into the infected animal's cage and gently pulls it out and sets it on the table. He gives the animal one of the injections.

He repeats the process with the clean animal.

Without warning the cancerous rabbit jumps off the table and falls to the floor. He quickly puts the healthy female rabbit away and goes to retrieve the other.

As he reaches down to pick up the animal, he stops himself and pulls back curiously as he sees the subject begin to twitch and twist on the ground. Then, as its hair begins to darken and bald spots begin to fill in, Jason hurries to pick the rabbit up and put it back into its cage. It's now quickly begun to bulk up and its eyes turn a cloudy, bloodshot yellow.

At first it doesn't appear to be aggressive, just thirsty and growling unusually. Jason reaches in to refill its spilt water tube and the mini beast lunges at his hand, barely missing his finger.

"Son of a bitch," Jason says under his breath as he pulls back, "You almost got me didn't you? I wonder if a little more would fix that attitude."

He proceeds to inject the rabbit with another dose of his serum, only this time through the cage. Again, it almost instantly begins to react, bulking up now even bigger than before. Its skin stretches and turns a dark shade of gray and now its veins rise to the surface. The little beast finally begins breathing slower, as it seems to be calming down and in more control.

The spectacle of it all has Jason concerned for what might be happening to the insides of his mutated specimen.

"Sorry little buddy, I'm afraid I am going to have to see what kinds of internal effects this stuff has had on you.

He prepares for the autopsy by injecting the little monster with a dose of an anesthetic, a serum meant to euthanize the animal.

But it doesn't die.

He prepares a second dose and injects it again and the animal isn't fazed.

Confused, he sits back to think about his finding. In walks both Alexis and Addy who is carrying a foil wrapped plate of food.

"Hey, Uncle Jason." Alexis says with a grudge in her tone.

"So, she's still mad at me?" Jason asks really not caring about the answer and instead seeming more concerned with what they brought him.

"Furious." Addy adds, "She won't stop going on and on about it."

Alexis gives Addy a glare from across the room as she sets the plate she brought on the back counter. Jason removes his gloves and walks away from the cages.

"Well, her dad will be home soon. We'll see what he has to say about it." Jason says as Addy walks past him and over to the cages.

Alexis pouts by plopping herself down on a stool.

Meanwhile, Addy opens the healthy rabbit's cage just long

enough to pet it gently. She then moves over to the other beastly animal's cage while Jason wasn't looking. She lifts the cancerous rabbit out.

"Don't be scared little guy." She whispers into its floppy ear, "What did my uncle do to you?" she adds lifting the mutated rabbit up to look into its eyes.

Jason turns with a mouth full of pasta and notices Addy snuggling with the animal.

"No, not that one!" He forces the words out through the food in his mouth, startling Addy.

"Why? He's not going to hurt me." She says as she continues to snuggle with it.

Alexis stands and starts towards her, "Put that ugly thing away, it's creeping me out."

Addy quickly lifts it up higher and into Alexis' face, forcing her to squeal. Meanwhile, the infected rabbit, being startled itself, relieves itself all over Alexis' hands, shirt, and shoes.

Standing there disgusted and at a loss for words, out of nowhere everything in the lab begins to rumble, forcing everyone to grab hold of something sturdy to keep from losing their balance.

Seemingly unfazed by the shaking, Jason's mind is still focused on the problem.

"It took a massive dose of the serum for the beast to become docile again and now it has no reaction at all to a lethal dose of anesthetic that could put down a horse?"

"Jason? Uncle Jason!" Alexis impatiently tries to get her uncles attention.

"Yeah?" He replies snapping out of it.

"What is that?" she asks as the tremors continue.

"I don't know." He answers quickly taking the animal from Addy and locking it up as they all head outside.

The sun is bright, and being inside all day has forced Jason's eyes to adjust to the brightness. Then, just as the rumbling begins to subside, he sees that the rumbling is from a massive train that is now creeping to a stop. The train is loaded down with strangely familiar, oversized containers. He also notices each one is equipped with special electronic security locks and heavier than normal doors.

"That's a really long train." Addy says grabbing her uncle's hand.

"Yeah, it is." Jason adds looking down the horizon at what looks like an infinite train, "Why don't you and your sister head home and don't make any stops."

CHAPTER FOUR

THE HIGHWAY SIGN READS:
KINGMAN CITY LIMITS

Michael and Cindy blow past the highway sign doing 75 mph, when they are abruptly forced to slow down. When they reach the main strip of small businesses that line the street at the entrance into downtown Kingman, they are at a crawl.

"I know what I want." Michael says pulling onto the adjacent Route 66 turn off.

"What?" Cindy asks.

"A real, old fashion American cheeseburger and some fries from the old diner." He perfectly times his reply with pulling into the parking lot of the town's oldest diner, "Let's grab a few orders and bring them home to my girls."

Next to the diner is a little park that the townspeople have nicknamed the "train park." It is home to an old decommissioned locomotive that sits as a centerpiece for the downtown area and a symbol of the fact that Kingman is the first major stop for trains heading out from the west coast. As always, there is a small crowd of tourist gathered in front of the train and snapping pictures while children climb through it.

Across the street and behind a strip of buildings is the towns actual train station which is accented by a huge water tower that sticks out as the tallest structure in town, besides the oversized wind farm propellers back in the distance.

As Cindy slams her door shut, they make their way towards the front of the restaurant. Michael looks over and notices the massive train stretching for miles. He stops and pulls up his sunglasses to get a clearer view at what has caught his eye.

"Hey sis, do you see that?"

"What?" she replies.

"You see all those train cars with the heavy-duty electronic doors?"

She looks, but just shrugs him off.

Michael continues, "They're military grade. We used them for transporting extremely hazardous material out of contaminated war zones or disaster areas. Why are they here and why are there so many of them here?"

"I thought you were hungry?" Cindy interrupts.

"Right, sorry." Mike replies.

Cindy tugs him by his shirt sleeve and leads him into the diner.

Meanwhile, at the train yard, two filthy rail workers in over-worn coveralls are standing side-by-side scratching their heads, confused about the train.

"Where the heck do you think this thing came from?" one

asks the other.

"I have no idea." The other one responds as he examines the electronic locks closer.

"What I'm wondering is, what it's hauling that requires locks like this and why whoever it is needs this much of it?" He continues as he looks down the line.

The first man climbs up to where the engineer should be.

"There's nobody in here?" He yells down.

"Well then, who the hell's driving this thing?"

The red lights on the first containers lock changes to green and the heavy lock clicks releasing the door. A hiss of gas is released like popping a fresh soda can, just as the seal on the container is broken. Then, the automatic door engages and slides open all the way with a clang.

The worker up on the train jumps down and joins his partner who is now staring into the darkness of the container.

Slowly from the darkness emerges a very attractive pair of long legs wearing tight khaki shorts. They're followed by a fit, bare stomach that leads up to a full and voluptuous tank top covered chest.

"What the hell is she doing in there?"

"I have no clue. Maybe she's part of some illegal sex trade?"

"Why does her skin look like it's discolored?"

"I don't know maybe she's been locked in here a while?" He adds acting cocky and grabbing at his collar as if to straighten himself up, "I'm going to go see if she needs a hand."

As he takes a step forward, so does the woman, only now her face has finally made its way into the light, exposing her lip-less face and yellow, bloodshot eyes.

"What the...?" is all the worker gets out before, from each side of the dead woman leaps two blood-thirsty runners who pounce almost straight through the men. The beasts begin to viciously maul into any part of the men's exposed flesh that they can sink their teeth into.

They are quickly joined by an out pouring of dozens of slower moving crawlers, as well as additional runners. From the back of the compartment, two sets of yellow eyes emerge as they make their way towards the doors opening.

The first one jumps down out of the car. He's a muscular dead man standing about 6'5" tall and dressed in old green German army fatigues. His teeth are bloody and he has heavy blue and purple veins that vine throughout steely skin.

In a raspy German accent he barks out a single order, "Tisim...enough!"

The rest immediately stop and turn their heads at the sound of his words. The large leader nods and passes the look up to the final dead who is now standing at the edge of the containers opening and obviously the one who is really in charge as he's got everyone's attention.

This smaller dead man is also dressed in military attire, only he looks to be of Japanese descent and has a large scar that runs vertically through his left eye leaving him with only one eye and an empty socket.

Everyone awaits his order.

"Open…the…next…box." He struggles to get out.

CHAPTER FIVE

"Alexis and Sam sitting in a tree, k.i.s.s.i.n.g..." Addy sings.

"If you don't shut up, I'm going to lock you in the closet." Alexis gripes.

Alexis is sitting on the bathroom counter, leaning in towards the mirror putting on eye makeup. Meanwhile, Addy is swinging on the door handle with her head back being as annoying as possible.

Alexis stops and smells her hands.

"Yuck, I took two showers and I used a half a bottle of apple wash and I still don't think I got all that crazy rabbit's crap off me."

Addy walks up behind Alexis so that she can be seen in the mirror; "You know you're not allowed to go anywhere."

"Shut up and mind your business." Alexis snaps.

"Uncle Jason said you're not allowed." Addy teases.

"Shut up, or else." Alexis warns.

"Or else what? It is my business, Uncle Jason said you're supposed to be watching me."

"Dad will be here in a couple of hours and I'll already be gone night. So what if I get punished after that." She shrugs.

"You're bad."

"That's what I want Sam to say!"

"Gross!"

Suddenly, from outside, there's a series of honks that make Alexis perk up and Addy confused.

They take a second to look at each other, and then both run over to the window to see who it is.

"Ooooh, I'm telling." Addy says turning and walking away.

"Come on, you can play in my room? You can play with my make-up or whatever you want?"

"Nope, I'm telling."

Frustrated, Alexis stomps her foot into the ground and chases Addy out of her room.

They continue running around the house until Addy ends up bolting into the deep walk-in closet that sits at the end of the hall. The slamming of the door causes the door to lock. Alexis doesn't notice that the closet door locked and decides to give up the chase and instead grabs her hoodie on her way out the front door to meet her friends.

Left alone and locked in the closet, Addy begins to pound on the door, "Let me out of here! I'm telling dad on you!"

Al hears Addy's pounding and begins scratching and sniffing at the closet door until he finally curls up at its base.

Meanwhile, outside the diner, Cindy and Michael have got their order and are heading back to the truck.

Suddenly, a female scream comes curdling from across the street, in the train yard.

"Get in the car." Michael says.

"Why? Let's just call the sheriff." Cindy says concerned.

"They won't make it in time." Michael adds running off towards where he hears the screams coming from.

He turns into the alley where he grabs a broken table leg from a pile of furniture stacked next to an old store.

As he prepares to turn the final corner he hears the faint sound of the woman who's now moaning. But, for the first time, he also hears the grunting and growling of dozens of others at well. He decides to peak around the corner before jumping out. What he sees shocks him.

He sees the two bloody, motionless bodies of the train workers and the woman he heard makes a third and they are now being hovered over by the crowd of cannibalistic monsters.

He decides he needs a plan to draw them away from the mangled bodies when, all of a sudden, the first two bodies start moving and slowly get up. Michael breathes a sigh of relief because he thinks the two have survived. Until they quickly join the others and each take a bite out of the woman.

Michael doesn't understand what he's seeing and it takes a minute for him to believe it.

"What the hell is going on?" he says to himself.

He peaks back around the corner and sees the third body being drug over to the opening of the first container where it's plopping down with disregard.

The leader barks out an unintelligible order and the crowd breaks up and disperses in different directions.

Michael knows he's out numbered and instead decides to attempt returning to Cindy. But, before he can go more than a few steps he sees they've already made it out to the streets behind him. He decides to go around the building the long way, but as he turns he doesn't see the women's body anymore. He doesn't have time to worry about it now and knows he has to get back to his sister before those things get to her.

He creeps his way out of the alley as quietly as possible, still gripping the thick wooden table leg.

All of a sudden, he's startled when he's cut off by the woman who is now a crazed, lip-less, and missing multiple chunks of her flesh. She appears to be moving in what can only be described as 'fast forward' and Michael is now trying to track her movements.

A slight pause in her erratic motion comes when she seems to be sizing him up. Then, without warning she charges at him viciously.

CHAPTER SIX

"He's been back three hours and he's already had to run off and be the hero." Cindy says to herself while fumbling around inside her purse. She's trying to find her keys, while still trying to keep an eye on where Michael went.

As soon as she's in the truck, she sees what looks like a man bolt past her. Then, there is another one and another as a group of them are now passing by.

"What the hell?" she says to herself looking for a cop or whoever it is that must be chasing them. Only instead, another one rips past her this time heading towards the diner's front door.

Immediately following these runners is a small group of the slower moving ones. It's only now she gets a good look at their disfigured faces and vein riddled gray skin. Her eyes grow wide as she begins to freak out and throwing the truck into drive, instead of reverse, pulls out of the diner parking lot over the curb.

She heads in the general direction she saw Mike go, but as she gets ready to pull into the alley next to the furniture store, she sees a gang of these dead monsters heading right for her.

"Where the hell are you?" She mumbles, still confused and not sure what to do next.

As she looks down the alley, in the distance she sees Michael's jacket on the ground covered in blood. She immediately thinks they've killed him.

"No, no, no, no." she begins to weep.

The gang of corpses closes in, forcing her to jam the truck into reverse just as they reach her. A fat one jumps up onto the hood and begins smashing at the windshield. Then, a crazed female torn from her belly button to her neck line jumps into the bed of the truck and begins pounding on the roof. From all sides they begin attacking until finally smashing out the passenger side window.

Cindy picks up speed and pulls the trucks wheel violently from side to side. This shaking knocks the pig off her hood. At this point, she slams on her brakes sending the crazy woman in the bed flying over the front of the truck. She slams the truck back into drive and runs over everything that has landed in her path.

Thinking she's in the clear, she begins to weep again. Suddenly, something in her rear-view mirror catches her eye. She sees she's being chased by a wild-eyed runner who is now rabidly in pursuit. But, just as she passes through one of the towns typically busiest intersections, she runs a red light. At that exact moment the dead sprinter in pursuit reaches out for her tailgate and is instantly splattered by a semi-truck that is crossing the intersection at the exact moment.

Thinking that he just murdered someone the truck driver stops, blocking the road, and gets out of his truck.

Within seconds more dead have arrived, and from her rear-view mirror Cindy sees the trucker is quickly overtaken by the mob of cannibalistic killers.

THE ROAD SIGN READS:
WORLD FAMOUS ROUTE 66

Cindy is now heading instinctively towards home and
sobbing uncontrollably at the thought of losing her brother.

Her eyes filled with tears, she barely notices her husband
Jason passing her by heading in the opposite direction and
towards the monsters.

Panicked, she spins the truck around, almost losing control,
to head him off before it's too late, before those things get
him too. She races up next to him honking and wildly flailing
her arms trying to get him to stop.

He doesn't stop.

She speeds up passing in front of him and then slams on
her brakes forcing him to do the same. She gets out of the
tattered truck and runs up to the passenger door. As she
opens it, she realizes why he couldn't hear her horn. He
has his stereo volume is cranked up.

He clicks the stereo off.

"What the hell are you doing babe? Trying to kill us both?"

Cindy tries to catch her breath through her tears.

"Where's Michael?" Jason asks.

She can barely manage to speak.

"There's something going on downtown. There are these

people who should be dead and they're killing everybody."
She pauses and gets quiet, "I think they got Michael."

"What the hell are you talking about?" Jason asks confused,
"Get in!"

Jason puts his hand to her cheek and kisses her forehead
gently before putting the car in gear.

As they get within a few blocks from where the semi-truck
was attacked, Jason's car crawls to a stop.

"They just started attacking me up the road a bit and the
last one chased me up until that semi hit him. They got the
driver." She continues to weep.

Jason turns up a quiet street, taking a different route.

"Where are we going?" She asks.

"To the last spot you saw your brother." He replies.

"But, what about those things?"

"We need to know if they got him. He might just be held up
somewhere and need our help."

He turns back on the main road. There he gets his first
glimpse at the carnage.

There are two people, dressed like theater ushers, being
attacked by a small mob of killers. One is face down on the
sidewalk, and the other is bent over the metal bus bench
with her guts strewn about.

Even the town's sheriff has been drug out of his cruiser, its lights still flashing, and it looks like he's been overpowered by multiple attackers.

"What do we do, what do we do?" Cindy begins to panic.

"Just tell me where you last saw him."

Cindy points in the direction of the old furniture store on the other side of the train park. They make their way over behind the building, but as soon as they turn the corner they see Michael's jacket still lying there in blood. As they get closer they find the savagely beaten body of the female runner who initially attacked Michael. She has a wooden table leg sticking up out of her head.

Cindy cries and tucks her head down while Jason turns his car around to get them out of there.

"He's not here, and there's no body. He's a trained soldier." Jason turn's, "Hey, I know he's still alive."

Cindy peeks up, staring out the side window at the carnage.

Jason speeds away.

CHAPTER SEVEN

Far enough away from the devastation taking place downtown and almost home, everything begins to feel surreal.

"It looks clear out this far." Jason says out loud, "They haven't had time to get out past that part of town yet. It seems like they're concentrated on downtown for now."

Cindy is still silent.

When they arrive at the house and find that it's dark inside, Jason is concerned.

Inside, Al greets them full of energy and frantically trying to lead them to the closet Addy has been left in.

"What's up buddy?" Jason says to Al before yelling out, "Alexis and Addy? Is anybody home?"

By now, Al has grown impatient and is scratching at the closet door.

"What is it boy?"

Al continues to scratch at the carpet in front of the door until Jason finally opens it. He flips the light on and finds Addy curled up and sleeping on the floor. Al rushes in and begins to lick her face until she finally wakes up.

"Okay. Okay, I'm up."

"Addy? What are you doing in there and where the heck is your sister?"

"I don't know where she went. I was playing hide and seek with Al and accidentally locked myself in the closet."

Cindy breaks her silence, "Oh, no? What if she couldn't find her and went looking for her?"

Jason pulls his cell phone from his pocket and tries calling Alexis, but there is no answer.

He tries again, but still no answer.

"She couldn't of went far without a car and she knows Addy won't go anywhere without Al. You two stay here, I'm going to go look for her."

Meanwhile, the wind is whipping through Alexis' hair as her and her friends are cruising down a backstreet in a new convertible. Everything seems peaceful in the part of town they are in.

In the front seat, sitting awfully close to one another is Alexis' best friend Suzy and her obnoxious boyfriend Steve. The two take every free moment they can to make out.

In the backseat with Alexis is her punky, spike haired boyfriend Sam. Alexis looks down at her phone and sees her uncle calling. She looks worried, but just hits the ignore button and tucks her phone away in her pocket.

As the car passes by the movie theater Alexis asks, "Where are we going?"

Steve takes a minute from tongue fencing with Suzy, "My brother is the bartender at Andy's dive bar downtown. He said if we came down tonight, he'd let us drink."

"Sounds like a plan." Sam adds sliding Steve a slick high five.

"You're taking your seventeen year old girlfriend to a bar?" Alexis asks Sam.

"Yeah, well babe you're a lot older than that in here," pointing to her heart "and here," pointing to her brain "and here!" pretending to grab her chest.

"Uh, I am not that easy." She says slapping him and pushing him away from her.

"That's why we need to go to the bar." He mumbles under his breath.

Outside of the bar the street looks unusually calm. Nobody's walking or driving and when the teen's car pulls up to the bar, they all look around notice that it is somewhat odd that the streets are so empty.

"What's going on? Is there a party going on somewhere and we missed the invitation?" Suzy asks out loud to no one in particular.

"Oh, we're invited. And you, my dear, are the guest of honor." Steve says opening the door and trying to be funny.

Inside, it's more of the same emptiness. Steve's brother Billy is lying face down on the bar. He is motionless.

"Billy!" Steve yells out to his brother who does respond, "Hey, Billy!"

Still not getting a response, Steve takes his arm from around Suzy and gets a serious look on his face. He slowly steps closer and closer to his brothers still body.

"Billy?" He asks as he reaches out to shake his brother's shoulder, he is still unresponsive.

Steve looks back at his friends who all have looks of concern on their faces.

"Billy!" Steve asks only this time louder and with a more violent shake.

Suddenly, Billy jumps up and startles everyone.

"What the hell?" Billy say groggy and still out of it.

"You scared the crap out of me!" Steve says as a smile comes over his face and he punches his brother in the arm.

"Where the hell is everybody?" Sam asks.

"I don't friggin' know. I wouldn't be here either if I didn't live upstairs." Billy has poured himself a shot of vodka, "Looks like it's going to be another crappy night for tips." He says pausing to turn towards the girls, "So, these are the little friends you want to drink with? Where's mine?"

"Hey, come on now, we figured we'd drink a little beer, play a little pool, you know." Steve replies.

"Alright, alright, let me see your money." Billy asks.

Steve and Sam pull out whatever they have crumbled up in their pockets and set on the bar. Billy picks it up and looks it over before handing them a pitcher of beer and the keys to the lock on the pool table.

Steve quickly unlocks the table, while Sam pours everyone a beer. Sam hands the first one to Alexis, who just sits staring at it, while everyone else gets there's.

"Cheers." Steve clanks everyone's mug harder than necessary and they all take a drink.

Alexis takes a tiny sip and spits it out immediately.

"Eww, that's nasty!" She exclaims.

"I forgot you've never had beer before, babe." Sam say's putting his arm around her.

"Just drink it fast, that's what I do to get it down." adds Suzy.

Alexis takes a big gulp and forces the fermented brew down the best she can.

"There you go." Sam says before finally being able to kiss her.

Again, she pushes him away.

"I'm going to have to drink this crap just to wash 'you' out of my mouth." She says with a sarcastic smile.

The friends begin taking turns hitting the pool balls around the table.

Across town, inside the Kingman Movie Cinema's, Jason is going up and down the dark isles looking for Alexis.

"Alexis are you in here?" He tries to whisper loud enough to be heard, only to be shushed by somebody in the audience.

In the empty lobby, the manager is frantically trying to reach somebody on the telephone.

"Look, I don't know where you two are but its Friday night and you two are supposed to cover this late shift for me. Call me back or better yet just get your butts in here!"

She notices Jason standing in front of her and hangs up the phone.

"Hey, how is Mr. Jason tonight?"

"That's a tough one to answer today. Have you seen Alexis tonight?"

"No, and I would've since I'm the only one working. I tell you it's the last time I hire a married couple, cause when you lose one, you lose them both!"

"Where were they coming from?"

"They rent a room downtown, why?"

Jason flashes back to the scene when he was driving downtown and remembers the couple dressed in usher uniforms being attacked.

"There not coming and if you're smart you'll close early and get as far away from Kingman as possible. Something's going on downtown that might be spreading this way." He warns as he's heading out the front doors.

Back in the bar, Sam and Alexis are sitting in a booth Sam is lightly kissing her neck. The pitcher is empty and so are their glasses. The sound of the pool balls clanking against one another is being accompanied by the low volume of an old jukebox playing some ancient country song.

Without warning the front door is kicked in and the body of one of the sheriff's deputy's is thrown into the bar.

For a second nobody moves as he lies there lifeless appearing to have been mangled by something unnatural.

Then, Alexis pushes Sam off her and rushes over to the downed officer. When she gets to him, she pulls at his shoulder flipping him face up.

"Oh, my god!" Suzy gasps.

"This didn't just happen. These wounds have started to dry. Look at how the blood's all coagulated." Alexis states.

Billy picks up the phone to call the cops, but hesitates.

"What are you waiting for?" Alexis asks with a hostile tone.

"I've got a bar full of underage kids drinking on my watch, and I'm supposed to just invite the cops to start asking questions?"

Suddenly, what's left of the deputy's corpse rises up

infected. This startles everyone and causes Suzy to scream.

Sam pulls Alexis back by her collar, just as the dead officer takes a bite at her, barely missing.

Then again, the door is kicked in. Only this time it's blown off its hinges by the force and lands in the middle of the room. In walk two methodical looking beasts who are slowly sizing up the joint.

They decide to go straight for Billy, while the deputy continues his attack on the teens.

Steve has his pool cue in his hand and shoves it clean into the deputy's head, but he keeps coming. Then, Suzy swings and breaks a chair over the deputy's back, knocking him down.

Billy ducks down behind the bar to load the shot gun he keeps for emergencies. When he pops back up, it's just in time to shoot one of the slower ones in the stomach. It blows a visible hole through it.

He quickly cocks his gun and fires. His second shot hits the other crawler in the right leg, blowing it off completely.

Both beasts fall to the ground.

Everyone is out of breath and in shock at what they've seen and it's quiet for a second, except for the now eerie old country song playing on the jukebox. Everyone is looking at each other in shock.

Then, through the door steps the big one who gave

commands from the train. He first sniffs the air and then in a growl says aloud, "Tisim!"

One by one, the motionless bodies rise. Again they each gauge their prey and resume their attacks. At that moment, they're joined by the addition of two new grotesque runners who've rushed past the giant dead man standing in the doorway.

The faster ones both head right for the armed bartender. Unprepared, Billy barely has enough time to cock the shotgun when the first fast killer leaps over the bar just as he pulls the trigger and it blows the beasts head clean off. But it's too late, as the other quick son of a bitch hits its mark. In a single bite, it tears at him ripping his lips off while gouging out his eyes. The two wounded ones crawl on his fallen body to finish him off by tearing into his body.

Meanwhile, Steve and Suzy are wrapped up in a struggle with the deputy. One wrong move and the deputy bites clean through Steve's jugular. Blood sprays everywhere, hitting Suzy in the face and causing the floor to become slippery. She pulls back just enough to slip and gives the deputy's corpse enough of a position to turn and overwhelm her.

Witnessing the events in hiding, Sam sees an opportunity to attempt to drag a shocked Alexis out the back door.

The large leader hears the backdoor open and gets another whiff of the air as a breeze whips past the couple and into the bar. Attracted to the scent, he walks by Suzy and without concern rips her head clean off in a single swipe, her body still in the grasps the deputy.

He sniffs her neck hole but doesn't find what he's in search of and tosses it aside and continues towards the back door.

Alexis, being push by Sam, flies out the backdoor and has to catch herself as she lands on the ground from the momentum. Sam bends over to help her up, but just as he begins to lift her up, an arm bursts out and yanks him back into the bar.

Stunned, and unable to get to her feet fast enough, Alexis tries to crawl away backwards. The door flies open again, only now the large dead man steps out.

Again, he sniffs the air.

As Alexis begins to scoot away, he grabs her by the ankle. She struggles, but manages to get free leaving the monster holding only her shoe. He smells the stain on her shoe and quickly pulls his face away.

He curiously inspects the cowering Alexis and growls, "Go...or...die."

Startled at this chance she quickly scrambles to her feet and runs off down the alley with only one shoe on.

She rips across the highway and disappears into the overgrown brush.

CHAPTER EIGHT

A still sobbing Alexis is hysterically trying to escape, but because of the darkness in the desert, trips and falls down into the dirt. She struggles to stumble back to her feet as she tries to make her way down the dark road and away from the nightmare.

From the darkness up ahead she strains to see the distant headlights of a car heading towards her.

Rushing out into the middle of road she attempts to flag down the driver before it's too late. She's flails her arm in desperation as the vehicle creeps to a stop.

"Alexis Lynn is that you?" the feminine voice from inside the dark car asks.

"Yes, ma'am." Alexis answers getting close enough to notice it's the manager of the movie theater.

In her fluster, she fumbles with the door handle a second before getting it open and quickly getting in. She instantly locks the door and rolls up the window.

"What the hell happened to you? Your uncle was in the theater looking for you a little while ago? He's worried to death."

Looking around frantic, Alexis begins to explain herself. Unfortunately the words she's forming aren't coming out clear enough to comprehend.

The theater manager sits confused.

"Slow down honey, I can't understand you. It sounds like gibberish? Does this have something to do with what your uncle was warning me about?"

Not sure what her uncle might have said, Alexis takes a deep breath trying to compose herself.

"There are dead people killing everything they come across. They even got the sheriff and one of them told me to leave or it was going to kill me."

Confused, the driver leans her head towards the open driver side window. She takes a breath of fresh air and tries to process what she's just heard.

"Baby girl, are you on drugs? What did you take? You can tell me."

Out of nowhere the driver is ripped out of the car by her head.

Screaming at the top of her lungs, Alexis rushes to unlock the door and get out of the car.

Just as she's about to step off the concrete she glances back in the direction of the car to see if the thing was following her. Not paying attention to what is in front of her, she slams into something hard.

The surprise knocks her back off balance and back on her backside. When she looks up she sees she's ran right into the chest of her blood covered father.

"Daddy? Daddy!" Alexis exclaims in both relief and joy.

Just then, the runner jumps up onto the roof of the car and then down over it landing directly behind Alexis.

Its head, along with its left arm, is twitching at a blurring rate. It slows down enough to peer down at the fallen Alexis. As it pauses, Michael takes a hard swing at its head with another table leg that he's been carrying.

His blow knocks the monster back on and into the passenger side of the idling car.

It seems to be motionless so Michael turns to check on Alexis.

"Are you alright baby girl?"

"Behind you!" she yells.

Michael turns ramming a blade he's pulled from his belt, along with his fist, completely through the runners head and out the back of it.

"He was a scout for the others. That means more will be coming." He says pulling his arm out of the dead creature's skull.

"I'm so glad to see you!" Alexis whispers while clinching to her father.

The two get into the car and reverse out and towards home leaving the lifeless bodies on the dark road.

CHAPTER NINE

Jason pulls up in front of their house, frustrated.

Inside Cindy and Addy are gathering any and every type of weapon they can onto the kitchen table. Jason comes in with his arms full of tattered research papers.

He gives Cindy a look and shakes his head as he drops the load he's carrying on the couch, "I couldn't find her anywhere and she's not answering her phone."

"I just hope she didn't go downtown." Cindy adds.

"What's downtown?" Addy asks.

Just then, there is a jiggle of the door handle at the front door. The girls jump and grab for each other.

"Son of a..." Jason says grabbing an old samurai sword he's had on his shelf for years and prepares to fight.

Then, there is a knock.

Jason takes cautious steps towards the door until he's close enough to see out the peep hole. He drops his arms in relief and quickly opens the door.

Michael and Alexis walk through and almost in slow motion Cindy and Addy both run to them, clinging to their necks.

"We knew you were alive." Jason says to Michael while embracing his hand and giving his shoulder a hug, "We saw your jacket and the blood…"

Michael nods as he recaps the fight with the first dead he encountered and how he killed it.

"Well, after we heard the scream I went to help, but those slow zombie-like things had already chewed up these two rail workers and now were eating the lady I heard screaming. Then, whatever is leading them ordered them to all dispersed. When I tried to get back to Cindy, whatever the lady turned into attacked me. She was different, she was fast. I only think I got the jump on her because she was so new. After that, I realized that if you're going to get the fast ones, before they get you, you've got to aim for where you think they're going to be, not where they are. Otherwise you'll miss them every time. I killed a few more of the crawlers down the road, but they weren't fast like the other one, they were just tough. I had to practically dismember them before I got them to stop coming after me."

"One of their leaders talked and even let me go after he smelled something on my shoe." Alexis adds quietly knowing that if she tells her story about the bar she's going to be in trouble.

But, she does anyway.

Describing the talkers' reactions causes Jason to grab his data sheets and then look down at Alexis' remaining shoe. He sees a splotch were the medicated rabbit feces had left a stain.

"Addy, baby girl, go grab my black light."

"What's going on Jason?" Alexis asks concerned that

there's something wrong with her.

Addy returns and hands him his cordless black light. He flips it on.

"Hey babe, can you turn off the lights for me?" Jason asks Cindy.

Instantly it's revealed that Alexis still has a lot of the residue from the highly concentrated chemicals from the animal on her chin, neck, hands, and shoe.

"Eww, is that what's still on me?"

"Don't you see? This is what saved you. They don't like this chemical for some reason, it repelled them."

"I think I'm going to puke."

"So, if we could get more of this stuff we could repel them?" Cindy asks.

"Yes, but I have a better idea." Jason answers with his data sheets in hand.

"Girls go get ready for bed." Michael instructs them, "I'll come tuck you in, in a minute."

"How am I supposed to sleep?" Alexis asks.

"At least help your sister." Mike adds.

"I guess I better not take another shower." Alexis says in disgust.

"I wouldn't," Cindy adds giggling, "and be sure to give your sister some extra hugs tonight. Maybe some of that poop will rub off on her."

"Ha, ha." Alexis mocks sarcastically as she grabs her sister's arm.

"Can I sleep with you?" Addy asks.

"Yeah, come on."

Just as Alexis sits down on the bed, Addy jumps up onto her back pretending to choke her.

"What are you doing?" Alexis asks.

"You left me locked in the closet and went out with your friends. I'm mad at you."

It's at that moment Alexis actually takes in the fact that her friends are all dead, or worse now one of those things. She begins to weep uncontrollably.

Addy sees this and feels bad thinking she's the reason she's crying.

"It's alright Lexi, I forgive you." she says sweetly.

Alexis turns into her sister's arms and the two hug.

"I'm sorry." Alexis apologizes.

"It's alright." Addy pauses to take in her sisters words. "You know that's the first time I can remember you ever apologizing for anything."

"That needs to change."

CHAPTER TEN

DAY TWO

By all appearances the morning comes just as any other day would. There's a quiet peacefulness that isn't at all too uncanny in such a small town.

Addy rustles around pulling the covers up over her head until, she tosses and turns and kicks the blankets off completely to reveal that at some point in the night Al has climbed into bed with her.

"Did you climb in here to make sure you were close enough to protect us?" Addy asks cradling Al's face.

Alexis is already up and sitting at her vanity staring off though the glass and back into her own eyes.

"You feel any better?" Addy asks with her eyes barely cracked open.

She doesn't answer. So Addy spins her feet over to the floor and walks over behind her apparently comatose sister.

"Hey, you in there?" She asks now resting her chin on Alexis' shoulder and petting her hair.

"Yeah, I'm here. I just haven't been able to get the images of what those things did to my friends out of my mind."

"Sam?"

Alexis begins to slightly tear up, "Yeah, Sam."

"I'm just glad they didn't get you. Think about how sad I'd be staring at myself in the mirror if they'd gotten you." Addy replies.

Then, as if Addy unlocked something with her words, Alexis wipes her face and composes herself.

"Are you hungry? I'm making pancakes."

"Yes!" Addy exclaims pumping her fists.

The two head out into the kitchen where their uncle has engulfed the family's dining room table with paperwork. In its center sits his overworked laptop which, at this moment, is being clicked and tapped on in a fevered pitch. Jason is consumed with trying to figure out some sort of explanation.

Michael comes into the kitchen and sees his daughters beginning to cook and his brother in-law focused on his work.

"You know, with all this other stuff aside," Michael shares, "This is what I miss most when I'm gone. All of us coming together and gathering around dad's old, handmade oak table."

He pours himself some orange juice before taking his glass and heading over to the front window to assess the landscape. From the front window he's able to see traffic coming in any of the three accessible directions.

Cindy is hanging half sprawled off the couch, still asleep. Without warning, she snorts herself awake and jumps up frightened when she sees Michael's fixated.

"Are they coming?" She asks noticing his focus.

"No, it's quiet." He reassures her.

From the other room Alexis calls out, "I'm cooking breakfast!"

"Coffee, I need coffee." Cindy says as she stands and stretches. She goes to help the girls in the kitchen.

"Hey Jason, do you know these people?" Michael asks.

Jason pulls back from the table and extends his arms out in a prolonged stretch. He picks up his never used samurai sword and slides its sheath through his belt.

Outside the sight of a familiar couple apparently out for a walk in matching jumpsuits doesn't surprise Jason.

"Yeah, that's that new retired couple from up the street. They just moved here from California. They're out every morning at the same time doing their 5 miles."

"Don't you think we should warn them about those dead heads downtown?"

"Yeah, you're right, we better."

As the door cracks open, Al is the first to bolt through it.

From the porch Jason calls out, but doesn't get a response. Michael grabs a metal fence pole from an old pile of debris, just in case, as Jason steps off in the couple's direction.

"Hey! Mr. and Mrs. I forgot your names! Wait up!" He yells out again, "Hey!"

He continues yelling as he slowly jogs after them. After a few steps they finally slow to a stop. That's when Michael notices their heads are now twitching.

"Hey, sorry to interrupt your walk, but we have a little problem."

Jason waits for a response that never comes. The two snap around to reveal that they have been infected.

Their lips are gone and skin appears paper thin and riddled with intoxicated veins. Their hands and nails are torn up and bloody, probably from the initial battle that converted them.

Noticing that not-so subtle twitch, Michael instantly knows that they are both the fast ones!

"Oh, shit!" Michael says under his breath as the two turn and bolt right for Jason.

Then, as if the world regressed into some sort of slow motion scene, Michael hops off the porch and bolts over to intercept the two killers before they reach his brother-in-law.

Al, sensing the confrontation, takes an alternate route towards the two attackers.

As the two dead approach at full speed, Michael's timing is impeccable as he steps in front of Jason and shoves the metal fence pole right through the male's head. The fierce impact actually impales its brain out the back of its skull like a brain kabob.

Unfortunately, at that exact moment the woman reaches Michael just as Al leaps in to attack. She's able to scratch Michael with all four of her bloodied fingers deep across his face, just as Al bites into her arm dragging her down but in a circular motion.

Michael's face is torn down to the muscle, but he still manages to turn, following her path, to collapse her skull in one smooth motion with his fence pole.

He falls to his knees dripping blood.

The girls have been watching everything from the house and have now rushed out to his aid. Gasping and carrying on, they help Michael up and inside.

"How come some of them are so fast and others are slow?" Alexis frantically asks as they help her bleeding father into his recliner.

"Addy, baby, go grab me some plain white t-shirts and fill a pitcher of warm water and make it quick." Cindy's trying to be strong even though she's queasy at the sight of the pulsating wounds that now stripe her brother's face, "...And some peroxide too!" she yells out after Addy.

"I mean they seem to have their own frigging personalities. What kind of monsters are these?" Alexis continues ranting as she quickly begins to lose it.

"The genetically planned kind." Jason mumbles peeking through curtains for signs of anymore of them.

"I thought something was too perfect about these things." Michael adds, "I mean they almost worked in ranks and the big blonde one yelled something that they all listen to. Even the workers they had recently attacked. It's like it's encoded in them."

Addy returns with the supplies, but with all the talk Cindy's now begun to show her stress and is frantically trying to hide it by focusing on the wounds.

"Are you alright Aunt Cindy?" Addy asks innocently.

"No baby girl. It feels like the end of the world and we are talking about zombies."

Al nestles up against Addy's leg right in between her and Cindy.

"Don't worry Aunt Cindy, Al will protect us."

Cindy snickers and the two lean in and touch foreheads. Addy looks down and lifts Al's chin, "Right boy." she asks semi-playfully.

It's then that she notices that Al's tongue and lips have begun to lose their color and bluish green veins are spreading throughout them.

Minutes pass by like a blink of an eye and while Michael is sitting back with the wet cotton cloth on his wounds, he's listening to the banter. Flashes of different thoughts race through his mind.

Then he catches a whiff of an unusual odor that he's never

smelt before.

Suddenly, from the kitchen table, Jason has an epiphany about the origin of the dead monsters and their chemical makeup, "I've got it!"

Michael now sniffs the air again, only this time harder and its apparent he can smell something no one else can, and it reeks. He peels off the cloth that is now sticking to his face in some of the dry parts and it begins to slightly bleed again.

"I think I've got a solution," Jason says out loud, "I think I've already solved this thing if it is what I think it is. But, I can't know for sure until I get back to my lab."

Addy looks at her father, who is now sitting up and she sees that the same green veins spidering through Al's lips and tongue, are now beginning to show in her dads face. Not knowing what to say, she just sits and stares. Alexis notices the look on her sister's face and looks over at her dad.

"Dad?"

"Yeah, sweetheart?"

"You need to look at your face."

Concerned, he gets up to his feet and looks into the large mirror that hangs over the couch.

"Oh boy, this isn't good."

"Dad?" Addy adds, "Al's got it too."

Michael bends down to look into Al's now cloudy eyes and pale lips.

"We need to get to my lab." Jason says, "The two of them don't have much longer before they turn."

"What's at the lab?" Michael asks.

"Let's just say, I now know what we're dealing with and I think I can stop it or at least slow it down."

"But, your lab is minutes from downtown?" Michael asks stating the obvious problem with that plan.

"I know."

"How are we supposed to protect ourselves that close to the epicenter?" Cindy asks.

"Chemistry and guns, but we got to go now." Jason answers definitively.

They all agree and without hesitation grab all the weapons they can carry from the house.

On the road, as they approach the area of town where the lab is located, they see that the streets have become overrun by roaming dead.

"What are they doing up there?" Cindy asks pointing up towards the skyline.

"There cutting the phone lines so we can't call for help." Jason says slamming his hand on the wheel, "They couldn't knock out all the phones, just the land lines down here. Plus, we still have the new cell phone tower." Jason explains pointing up to it.

Just then, in the background, the tower begins to sway back and forth.

"Dad?" Addy asks.

"Yeah, baby girl?"

"The new cell phone tower is coming." She answers as the tall tower begins to topple over.

Jason is forced to slam on the brakes and swerve up onto the side walk to avoid being crushed as the massive tower crashes down directly in the trucks path.

"What the hell is this?" Jason says puzzled.

"Calculated, that's what it is." Michael responds feeling the effects of the infection spreading.

As the truck creeps through the street filled with the familiar faces of the recently undead, it's quickly surrounded. The persistent crawlers and rabid runners begin to pound the truck. It only takes seconds for a dozen or so of them to begin throwing themselves onto the vehicles sides and up on its roof.

"Jason, we got to ram through them." Mike groans in a new, painful tone.

Turning to see Michael is wrenching at his chest, Jason begins smashing into parked cars and scraping against concrete walls, crushing the monsters and knocking even more off and onto the street behind them.

As they turn the corner that leads to the lab, the truck has been cleared off. Unfortunately, there is a crowd building up and chasing behind them.

Jason yanks the wheel and slides the truck as close as he can to the building to give them a straight shot in.

Jason jumps out of the truck and with sniper like aim slams the key into the doors lock. The truck doors kick open and they all begin to rush in.

Mike and Cindy are the last ones out of the truck. Behind them, the mobs of dead are rushing for them as fast as they can, with a few runners out in front leading the way.

Cindy, in her haste, takes a wrong step and trips and falls to the ground. Just then, the first runner clears the truck in a single leap.

Al leaps between them and the killer to ward off the attack and is almost instantly bitten. This gives Michael the time he needs to rush over and help her up.

Just as she reaches the door, the same initial runner dodges Al long enough to get one last swipe at her, scratching her deep down her back.

She instantly lets out a scream that triggers Michael's reflexes causing him to turn and swing with such force it literally caves in the monsters head.

Just as he begins to slam the door shut, Al dives through

limping.

CHAPTER ELEVEN

The door locks and the men begin grabbing for anything they can use to reinforce it. Nothing seems to be working. The dead keep coming and are now throwing themselves against the door and the surrounding walls.

"Back up." Michael says stepping behind the soda machine that stands next to the door. With one push he tilts it over enough that it falls over barricading the door with enough weight to hopefully hold it for a while.

Jason lifts Cindy up, being careful of her back, and carries her into the kitchen and lays her down on the table.

Alexis pulls the first aid kit off the wall and opens it up pulling out item after item to begin treating the wounds.

"Go make sure they can't get in." Cindy tells Jason, "I don't want those things to get in and get the girls."

Jason rushes to the back door and sees that it is already chained up.

"Let me see what we've got." Michael says with a groan.

"Are you alright? You're starting to look really bad." Jason asks.

"No, but let's keep moving. That seems to help."

He leads Michael to a metal closet and unlatches it. As the doors creaks open, he reveals an armory full of machine guns, grenades, and ammunition.

"All this for a lab?" Michael asks.

"A government lab in disguise." Jason answers.

"And never even a word?" Mike asks.

"Never came up." Jason answers.

Jason leaves Michael to assess the weaponry and heads to his lab stopping by the kitchen on his way.

"How are you, babe?" He asks.

"I'll be alright. Just fix this before I start getting hungry for brains." Cindy says making comical zombie hands in Addy's direction trying to lighten things up for her young niece.

Addy half giggles, but Alexis shoot her a look that kills it.

"Alright." He says giving her a deep hard kiss before continuing on his way.

Inside the lab, Jason pulls from the refrigerator the large vial of his formula he was working on last. He adds a couple of elements from a few different shelves and places the bottle into the centrifuge.

He turns and sees that the original rabbit specimens are still alive and don't appear to have changed any further. He looks closely at the mutated specimen and sees that it has remained docile.

Wanting to make sure, he pulls the clean rabbit from its pen and puts it in with the other.

"Let's see how you act with your first love, buddy."

The two just sniff each other.

"Well that's a good sign." he says to himself as a bell dings signaling the mix is complete.

Once the device stops its cycle he prepares three doses of the light green formula. He then continues working as fast as he can.

He pulls a portion of the mix from the existing vile and runs it through another machine. He prepares three more syringes of the now dark green solution.

Grabbing up all the syringes he returns to the kitchen where Michael is handing out guns and ammo. Cindy is now sitting up.

"Well, I've got good news and bad news."

"What do you mean bad news?" Cindy asks.

"Well, the good news is I think I've created a working vaccine."

"And the bad?" She asks again only this time more persistent.

"The bad news is that you guys are going to turn into something like those things out there really soon."

Cindy gasps and leans her head into Jason's chest and the

girls rush over to hug their father.

"But, I think I've been able to create a serum that seems to allow you to remain in control of yourselves. Only it might have some physical side effects that I can't predict."

At that moment the doors again begin to savagely be pounded by the dead's outside desperate to get in.

"They really want in here." Alexis says.

Jason injects Michael with the first syringe an waits a moment worried about a reaction. When nothing happens, he has another thought and hands a few of the syringes to Michael.

"You inject the girls and Al and I'll get Cindy."

Al goes into a corner and lies down as if he feels he's in trouble. Michael leans down and pulls a handful of loose skin and administers the drug.

Like the rabbits, it only takes a minute before the combination of infection and new serum begins to take effect. Sensing this he curls up and rapidly begins to bulk up to more than twice his size and his breathing seems to turn into a demonically deep growl.

Addy breaks away from her sister and holds her mouth at the sight of her best friends transformation, but with tear filled eyes approaches him anyway.

"No! Addy don't go near him!" Alexis yells.

She continues towards him until Michael grabs her. She

struggles free and pushes his hands away.

"No dad, it's Al. He won't hurt me."

Taking a deep quivering breath he reluctantly lets her go.

"Be careful baby girl. This is new to him too."

She reaches out her hand to her now monstrous looking friend to smell.

"Michael?" Jason says.

"I'm on it." He replies lifting his weapon and pointing it directly at Al's forehead.

Addy bends down and extends her hand closer. After a quick sniff, Al begins to lick it through his now elongated teeth.

Everyone in the room exhales with relief.

Now, the focus turns to Cindy as Jason injects her. They wait. She doesn't show any signs of changing after a few minutes, so he draws a sample of her blood with the same syringe and rushes back to the lab and his microscope.

Everyone follows him.

Focusing hard into the lens he makes a discovery.

"Her cells are not being affected?" He says excited, "Maybe it has something to do with being female? Or maybe it's something in the female DNA that works with the serum to counter act the side effect?"

"Could the fact that I'm pregnant affect it?"

"Whoa, babe you're pregnant?" Jason pulls her close to him and kisses her and places his hand on her belly.

"I wanted to tell you at a better time, but all this…"

"No. It's alright babe."

Cindy nods.

"That must be it." Jason answers after a few seconds of shuffling the pages that are strewn about the table.

A crash from the front door draws everyone's attention as the continuous pounding has begun to work and the doors are starting to give.

Jason and Michael rush out to check if they've been able to breach the entry.

"You know we have to fight now, it's only a matter of time." Michael proclaims.

"I know."

Jason rushes back to the lab and pulls out the tray from under the infected rabbit that is now breeding with the other rabbit.

"Glad that still works." Michael jokes standing in the doorway while Jason empty's the waste into a large glass beaker. He proceeds to mix in a few other chemicals in and then separates everything into several other smaller beakers.

Addy looks up and sees the veins on her dad's arms look incredibly painful.

"Daddy, you need to take another shot now."

Looking down at what she's staring at he agrees with a nod.

She asks, "What are you making with that rabbit stuff uncle Jason?"

"We're making zombie stink bombs." He explains adding more chemicals to the mix, "This will make them flash and cause the solution to become a gas on impact. Can you carefully cork them off for me baby girl?"

"Sure."

He returns to the vile of the darker green mixture and makes an additional dose of the drug.

Jason turns to see that Cindy's wounds have in fact, already begun healing.

"It's really working." A smile creeps over Michael's exhausted face. "It's working! We're going to need more." He half laughs.

Then a pain shoots through his body and up into his head. In that moment he knows he can't wait another second as his eyes begin to haze over.

Jason hands him two doses and nods. With two hands Michael slams both needles, one into each leg, and pushes the massive doses into his blood stream.

An instant rush of what could only be described as adrenaline shoots up the same path of his body and again into his brain.

"Get yourself and the girls up to the roof and get ready to fight!" He exclaims as he turns to rush himself into the adjacent bathroom.

The sound of him savagely thrashing around has everyone locked in a state of shock, but the cracking sound of the front door snaps them out of it.

They quickly pick up their weapons and make their way out of the room and up to the roof through the internal hatch.

CHAPTER TWELVE

Outside of the lab the dead continue to gather around the building, as the two leaders are standing off in the distance, apparently strategically assessing the situation.

The smaller Japanese talker motions to the larger one with a spin of his fleshless finger. Evidently he's instructed him to call every dead into action. The larger one has a look of discontent in his cloudy eyes. It's obvious he has distaste for being ordered around by the smaller talker. So, he first shrugs off the command and does nothing, essentially sending a non-verbally mutiny to his would-be commander.

"You…can speak. So…speak." The large one fumbles.

The Japanese talker takes a worthless deep breath extending and contracting his puffed chest. Then, out of nowhere, he reaches back and smacks the larger insubordinate hard across the face.

"Obey."

The large one takes it and from the recoil of the smack yells out, "TISIM!"

Out from the bushes and from around the corners every dead within an earshot begins to assemble. Dripping and scraping their way towards the building.

Meanwhile, up on the roof there are rows of machine guns lined up with spare clips neatly set in-between each gun as if a child had just set the dinner table.

Everyone, but Michael, is there preparing for war. Al is peeking over the edge of the building barking in baritone and sporting his new strengths to the beasts below.

Michael steps out onto the roof with a thud.
His once large frame has been dwarfed by what he's become. He stands nearly seven feet tall and hulking with the same familiar pale vein filled skin of the dead. His clothes now stretched to the brink of busting off his body. His eyes are yellowed and accented with ribbons of red blood shot running through them. His mouth is producing excessive amounts of saliva and his breathing his heavy and deep.

Addy is the first to turn around crying out, "Oh, no, daddy?" This causes everyone else to turn and gasp.

Jason raises his gun, "Is that you?"

Michael stands unresponsive at first. He has to collect himself internally. Then, to be reassuring, he bends to a knee and extends his arms out towards his baby girls.

"It's…me. I'm…in…here."

Both of the girls rush into their fathers arms and he embraces them momentarily before refocusing his attention to the fight. He is now towering over all of them as he walks out to the ledge to survey the battlefield.

"Toss…out…the…beakers." He gets out while pointing in different directions.

"What about you? Isn't this stuff going to affect you too?"

Jason asks.

"I don't think so…I'm…not like them." Michael's words begin forming easier. "Whatever you gave me made me different. I can smell our differences."

"Are you sure?" Jason asks.

"Yes."

Then, one by one they toss them out over the edge where they explode on impact with a flash and subsequent flow of noxious fumes. The dead don't know how to react, so they begin to withdraw.

The Japanese leader seeing this begins to yell incoherently, but when he doesn't see the same passion from his large underling, he reaches back to strike him again.

As he releases the blow it's intercepted.

"Enough!" The large one demands.

Back on the roof top, Michael takes a few steps back to give him enough room.

"I need everyone covering me to make this work." He says.

"Make what work?" Jason asks.

Without any warning, he runs and leaps off the roof and into the scattering crowd of living dead.

At first, no one attacks him as they see and smell him as one of their own, yet they sense something different.

The Japanese talker again instructs the larger one to gather the army. The larger one snarls and reluctantly agrees, but not before attempting to push the smaller beast back.

Unexpectedly he's sure footed and doesn't budge. Instead he glares at the larger one until he eventually seems to accept his role. He turns as ordered and howls out the order to attack.

"Tisim...enemy!" He points to Michael who stands ready to fight.

The fleeing dead stop in their tracks and turn as instructed.

The runners are the first to strike. Their fierce attack has them each flinging themselves at Michael in an attempt to knock him over. One after another they're batted away in all directs. Some get their slashes in, but for the most part they are pounded back.

From the roof, Jason tries to estimate their paths but his shots keep finding nothing but the dirt.

Then, in what looks like a moment of reprieve, the next wave attacks as dozens of crawlers completely surround the blood striped Michael.

From the roof top the beastly Al jumps down to join his master in the fight. He leaps at the throat of the first crawler who dares step out of the pack.

Their pace makes for easy targets and Jason lands shot after shot and is now joined by Cindy and Alexis with Addy reloading clips.

Bullet after bullet hits its target, but the beasts keep coming. Then in a fury, Michael begins to swipe the heads off each of the attacking crawlers leaving their bodies to flail on the ground. Al continues to fight off anything that attempts to sneak by unnoticed.

As if they're using the piling bodies as ramps, the runners resume their attack.

At first a few get through and one even takes a chunk out of one of Michael's arm before he crushes its skull. One by one they're swatted from the air landing hard on their backs.

This allowed the family on the roof to continue taking easy shots picking each one off just as they hit the dirt.

When the dirt settles two or three dozen have fallen but several more await standing in the distance.

Both Michael and Al are breathing heavy.

The Japanese leader finally deciding to do his own dirty work orders the rest, "Attack…building!" and then turns to the large one, "Get…Him!"

The Napoleonic leader turns and walks away from the fight without ever lifting a dead finger. Instead he disappears off the battlefield.

The large one sees this and momentarily hangs his head while shaking it. But before the dead reach the building, Al has retreated to put himself in-between the building and the ghouls who still refuse to get within 20 feet of it.

"It's the chemical cloud of haze from the bombs." Cindy yells as they keep pumping rounds into the crowd.

The dead just stand there growling at a distance. Then, while the crew on the roof has a moment, they notice that those left are mostly the town's people.

"Look it's the sheriff." Jason notices.

"And the diner workers." Cindy adds.

"There's Steven, Billy, the movie manager, and…" Alexis sighs at the sight of who she notices next. "…Sam?"

Down on the ground Michael and the German leader are circling each other ready to fight.

At first the two swipe at one another landing a few harmless blows. Then, the talker leaps up throwing a downward elbow into Michael's upward looking temple. He follows it with gorilla-like two-fisted pounding the drives Michael to the ground face first.

Getting one foot planted underneath him Michael throws himself up propelling his hard head into the chin of the dead thug.

This move opens him up to be in the perfect position for Michael to grasp him by his neck. He twists to flip him over onto his back into the middle of a pile of cinder blocks.

Then, as if back in high school, Michael wrestles the undead into an arm bar that allows to easily flipping the beast over so he can take control of the monster from behind.

Michael is in position and ready to rip the oversized zombies head off, but the beast cries out, "Wait."

"Wait? Wait for what?" Alexis says to the others on the roof, "That's the one that let me go."

"I…don't…believe in fight. We've…been forced." He says as the flesh on his neck begins to split as Michael continues to pull, "That…is…not leader. Was forced…by…old man."

"Old man? What old man?" Michael asks.

Lying their helpless, the soldier reveals a rumor that the "Nazi" was some old feeble scientist who got stuck trying to find a solution for a cure to the many health problems that plague him. When he started running out of time, he tricked the world into helping him to complete his research and development. The hidden truth was that all the while they were building him a new army.

Jason searches his memory back to when the formula was first delivered to him by the military big shots and the old German doctor.

"That old son of a bitch was planning this all along!" Jason says to himself, "He's not lying!" He yells.

Putting his face next to the soldiers with authority Michael asks, "Where is he now?"

"Here, on…the…train! The…other one…went to…free him. To…enact…plan…Z."

CHAPTER THIRTEEN

As the Japanese dead approaches the last container of the train, it's different than the others. Instead of an electronic lock this one has a keyhole.

He slices his own chest and digs in deep, ripping past the flesh and organs. This digging becomes excessive, just as he finds what he's hunting for. He pulls his bloody hand out to reveal a key. He inserts it, still dripping, into the lock.

Meanwhile...

"What's plan Z?" Michael asks applying pressure to the back of the beast's head as he continues to struggle face down.

He continues confessing details with the hopes of saving himself.

"If...mission...failed...at any point...along the track...Nazi would...unload...the...whole train and...unleash...the...dead apocalypse."

"How many more dead?"

"The...containers...he'll release...ten thousand...dead soldiers, maybe more."

Michael looks worried as he sees the advancing dead encroaching closer and closer on the building.

"Where would they go?" He asks.

"Alternative…target. Recruit…soldiers."

"Where exactly?"

He hesitates and so Michael begins to pull back on his neck from behind lifting his chin to the sky.

"Las…Vegas. Las…Vegas!" It barely gets out through his mashed together teeth. He is no match for the chemically superior Michael.

Pissed that this is far from over and with the new blood coursing through his veins, Michael begins to rip the beasts head off from behind. With no time left, the dead gets out one last plea.

Straining to talk, "I will help…you!"

A breeze picks up and the gas around the building begins to dissipate.

The dead resume their push and begin to draw near the building again. Some even begin climbing.

Al begins to attack those closest and Jason hangs over the ledge shooting as many as he can, but there are too many.

The dead version of Sam makes his way over the ledge and heads right for Alexis.

"Sam, no, don't." She whimper's lifting her weapon and preparing to reluctantly fire at her former crush. Only, before she can fire, he lunges at her biting through her arm causing her to drop her weapon.

Cindy turns to fire, but her weapon needs reloading. She throws it down and leaps for Sam forcing him to release her arm.

A second dead makes its way up onto the roof and has begun pushing Jason over the edge of the building, while others are pulling him from behind. Addy is curled up in a ball at the back of the roof.

"I…can stop them." the large one pleads.

"So stop them."

"Let…me up."

Reluctantly, Michael releases its throat and helps him up by its arm. Only he never let's go of the back of his neck, just in case.

He takes a deep breath and yells his command "Tisim!" and the dead turn, dropping off the building and standing even more lifeless than they already are. Jason twists his hip tossing his attacker off the building.

"They'll…listen…like I promised."

Michael shakes his head, reluctantly.

"I can help all of you to be more in control and to be stronger. But, that means you're going to help to stop those on the train."

The dead leader extends his hand like he would when he was living, desiring the consummate bond of a hand shake.

Michael looks up to the roof and sees his girls leaning in on his sister, Alexis holding a bloody arm, but smiling. Jason gives him the thumbs up with one hand and holds up a machine gun in the other.

He grabs the dead man's palm and with a firm grip shakes it with a hearty tug, as the red of the twilight sky meshes with the few remaining streaks of blue.

Then, without warning, an abrupt and powerful pulse from an advanced electromagnetic blast tears through Kingman. The wave blows out street lights and fry's everything electronic for miles. The rapid dropping of the sun disappearing behind the ridge leaves everything and everyone in the dark.

TO WHOM IT MAY CONCERN:

It's been weeks since we returned to the train yard and found it empty. Weeks since the blast intended to quite us from warning anybody of any appending doom succeeded.

The immunization has worked better than we had hoped and Alexis has adopted the beneficial traits of the formula that rapidly healed her wounds.

Jason has been able to produce more serum and has treated the remaining 72 dead with it. Most have regained some sense of who they were and what happened. Unfortunately a few of them have tried to commit suicide not wanting to live like this. I hope they'll come around, because we're going to need them.

The rest have gained strength and have agreed to join us in defending those we can in Las Vegas, before it's over ran with those things.

Listen to me, "those things" I am one of those things now and that alone would be fuel enough to have me cross the desert.

But now, it's much more.

What kind of world am I leaving for my girls if we don't stop them somehow?

Not to mention I'm going to be an uncle soon. There's so much to worry about that I don't know what we'll do if we're too late.

We plan on leaving soon and being that we're in Kingman

we've been able to gather a few dozen horses and an old diesel military mover that was in pieces up until the blast that fried all our modern vehicles.

Hopefully we'll find somebody left in Laughlin or Boulder City on the way, or at the least find a way to communicate with Vegas before it's too late.

If we can somehow head them off by contacting the soldiers at the Air Force base, they could set up some sort of offensive before it's really too late for everybody."

Michael - infected soldier, father

A SIGN READS:
WELCOME TO LAUGHLIN, NEVADA

Neon lights flashing, cars honking, and people walk the street with their smart phones attached to their ears. Suddenly, an all too familiar blast pulses in the night sky and a massive wave of energy races through the town frying out light after light.

The whole city goes dark in an instant.

Block by block the screams begin.

A SIGN READS:
WELCOME TO BOULDER CITY, NEVADA

BELOW IT ANOTHER SIGN READS:
LAS VEGAS 20 MILES

Again that familiar blast and wave rips through the small town as everything goes dark.

A KNOCKED DOWN SIGN READS:
LAS VEGAS CITY LIMITS

A massive trail of footsteps in the dirt lead in the cities direction.

The swarms of tens of thousands of dead drag their way through the desert towards the tourist capital that's also home to over two million people.

Into the valley they march, led by the now transformed Nazi. He's wearing Alexis shoe on a rope around his neck. There's a piece cut from it where the stain used to be.

Meanwhile, the Kingman militia heads over the Hoover Dam, they see car after car has simply been abandoned.

In Boulder city, they find no one and it's the same thing everywhere.

As the militia breaks over the ridge to see the Las Vegas Valley, they pass the knocked down road sign and see the massive trail in the dirt leading towards the city.

They gather on the hill top and look out at the panoramic view of the Las Vegas valley.

They are revealed to a massive city that is now on fire and in chaos.

PART TWO

VEGAZ APOCALYPZE

TO WHOM IT MAY CONCERN,

My name is Alexis and I am writing this to warn you that our world has a new threat. Only it's not what you might expect.

The enemy is unlike anything we've ever seen before. These horrific undead creatures are both fast and fierce and some seem almost impossible to kill, while others show a military leadership that almost destroyed us all.

And it's not over yet.

The initial attack on our small town failed because my uncle, a chemist, was able to vaccinate us. He used his version of the serum to allow my father to regain control of his mind after he was attacked by one of the ones we now call "runners" and his mutation helped him to defeat the first wave of attacks.

My uncle's solution worked on my aunt Cindy, my sister Addison, and myself and a side effect from it allowed us to develop a remarkable healing factor that saved both me and my aunt's lives.

It didn't work as well on the males that had already been infected. Instead, it only gave them a fighting chance to remain in control of their minds.

This loss forced the enemy to move on to what they called plan "Z" which we found out means their commander was to release the entire undead army from their train cart cages with the mission to overtake the nearest heavily populated city. For us, that city is Sin City, Las Vegas, Nevada.

Although this time, it seems the infected aren't making the same mistake they did with us and instead of trying a sneak attack with only a few train cars full of dead zombie soldiers; they're bringing enough killers to bring on the beginning of what might be the apocalypse.

He's got tens of thousands of these monsters and even more being converted along the way. We know this, because we're on their trail and have found nothing but empty, blood soaked streets in the few towns along the way. Though it's not just the growing army that has us concerned for the massive Vegas valley, it's the other weapons he has that we fear can unbalance things and throw millions of unsuspecting victims into an all-out riotous frenzy.

We already know about the electromagnetic pulse device that fries anything electronic within several miles of it and it had kept us from warning anybody who'd believe us.

But what else do they have?

I know they have my shoe. It was stained with the serum from the original experimental rabbit and it's possible they could use it to figure out what my uncle did to adjust the formula and possibly treated themselves and maybe others by now.

Regardless, as we came up over that ridge leading into the valley, we saw that the fight for Vegas has already begun.

God help us all.

Alexis, mutant...dead survivor.

CHAPTER FOURTEEN

The desert night is quiet and the clear skies are glowing from the overabundance of neon and light coming from the inner city. The non-stop flow of passenger planes in and out the twenty-four hour city; fill the sky with hundreds of manmade shooting stars.

Just outside the North Las Vegas city limits, the impenetrable darkness that is the landscape is now slowly moving like an omnivorous wave flowing up onto a beach. Only this wave isn't pulling back into its source and instead continues to quietly proceed. In its path lies the pride of the American Air Force, Nellis Air Force Base. The thought of a ground attack may have been planned decades ago, but no one ever thought they'd ever really need enacted it.

And so they sleep.

After all, this base is land-locked, surrounded by mountains, and home to the best fighter pilots in the world. Who alive would be stupid enough to try to attack them on their home turf?

Not anyone alive, that's for sure.

Meanwhile, at the front gate two soldiers stand guard at the symmetrical entrance, one on each side of the small square guard booth.

Around the rest of the base there are only a few patrols making routine rounds. No one seems to be noticing anything out of the ordinary. They are especially unaware of what's creeping towards them in the night.

A truckload of off duty officers makes its way to a sloppy stop at the checkpoint. The driver appears to be the only one of them that is sober. He's being bumped by the guys in the backseat, who are wrestling around pretending to fight with one another.

"Sir!" The young guard snaps out as he stiffens up to a salute when he sees who the driver is.

"Airmen..." The obviously higher ranked officer replies with a lazy two fingered salute off his eyebrow. He squints to read the guards name, "...Jones."

"Looks like you've had one hell of a night, sir." Jones comments.

"Not bad. We'll have to take you out with us sometime. Show you how the big boys do it."

"Yes sir." Airmen Jones responds ambitiously.

"Good. So everything quiet here?" The Chief Master Sergeant asks.

"Dead sir, nothing but tumble weeds and crickets." He pauses, "And, I'm not even hearing the crickets anymore."

Just then, the sound of what can only be described as some sort of sonic boom explodes with a fury, on the south side of the base.

"What the hell was that?" The Chief exclaims as he fumbles to slam his truck into drive. "Open the gate son!"

As the button is pushed to trigger the gate, the wave of energy fries out the controller and stalls the truck and everything in the area goes dark. Second and third blasts erupt almost simultaneously only a few seconds later. The blasts blacken out the rest of the base and surrounding communities.

"We're under attack!" The officer mumbles, "Those sons of bitches are hitting us right here, right now?"

The truck empties as the men seem to instantly sober up. They each grab machine guns from inside the guards shed. Not sure what they were up against, only some of them grab any extra ammunition and most only have a single clip.

They make their way into the base on foot, heading towards where they heard the closest blasts. As they approach the area near the runways, they're joined by several dozen other armed soldiers who've come to fight.

Glaring out into the night they see nothing.

"It's too dark!" Someone yells out.

"That blast fried everything! Even my goggles are out!"

"An electromagnetic blast could mean these planes aren't worth crap to us anymore!" Someone else exclaims.

"There! What's that?"

The moon and greenish glow of the city is providing just enough light to make out the outline of a wide stretching mass that's heading straight for them.

"What the...?" The Chief says to himself confused.

Then, in a sudden rush, the first wave of runners burst out of the darkness ripping into the soldiers.

Shots are fired by those further back, but it's useless. The sheer number of swift attackers has them over ran in minutes.

The blood curdling screams begin to echo throughout the base, as throats are torn open and skull fragments begin to be devoured.

Several of the younger soldiers try to turn and run, only to be kicked down from behind as they're swarmed by dozens of crawlers.

Now, because of their long journey, the dead don't stop their feasting to allow for any conversions to take place. Instead, they're feverishly forced to replenish themselves and their thirst by consuming their victims down to the bones.

It takes the undead less than an hour to devour every walking thing on the base. It happened so fast that not even a single mayday call goes out.

MCCARRAN INTERNATIONAL AIRPORT
LAS VEGAS, NEVADA

The sun threatens to break the horizon, as the already busy airport is in full swing.

Passengers by the thousands are arriving for the weekend. The sound of slot machines and celebrity voices doing public service announcements fill the air.

"Come on we're going to be late!" A young woman says to the young boy she's dragging by the hand behind her.

"Mom?" He asks starring off.

"Stop dragging your feet. Let's go."

"Mom?"

"If you don't stop fighting me I'm going to kick your little butt." She says stopping and turning to see what has her son's attention.

"Look." He says pointing out the large window that stretches the wall between two of the terminals.

"What is that?" She says to herself as she squints and steps closer and closer to the window.

Screams coming from the end of the terminal line have everyone's attention, as onlookers try to figure out what's going on. Then, just as fast as they've turned their heads, the mass outside the window has gotten close enough that the young woman and her son can now see the horror that approaches. It's hundreds of filthy, bloody, and rabid dead, whose numbers stretch as wide as the view will allow. They're sprinting right at the terminal with murderous intentions.

Meanwhile, the people down closest to the turmoil happening inside the terminal are pushing and climbing over each other to get away from the vicious attackers that have already made their way inside. The sudden clogging of fleeing bodies has the mother and son pressed up against the glass.

A runner leaps up on top of the unmovable mass of scared patrons. When the dead speedster reaches a particularly tall man, it grabs at his head with two hands and bites down on his skull until cracking in to it. He's followed up onto the heap of terrified bodies by more and more runners as the attack begins to take place from the shoulders of the crushing crowd.

Outside, the window is met with the thrashing of undead bodies desperate to break through.

The helpless mother and her son are pinned, face to face, with the decrepit figures that taunt and bite at them from the other side the security glass.

From the opposite side the airport, the overwhelming mass of monsters flow into the terminals for their devastating feast. In their path, they leave bodies bloody and twitching, gnawed and demolished. Then, without warning, the all too familiar sound of the sonic boom's blast tears down the runway. Its impression instantly immobilizes everything except for two flights that are able to leave the ground, each heading in opposite directions and just ahead of the blasts radius.

At that same moment, the pulses wave clashes up against the building causing the windows to splinter under the sudden pressure. The lights fry and all the slot machines sizzle to a silence, just as the long, people moving escalators grind to a halt.

A large stress crack begins to crawl down the window that is the only thing separating the young mother and her son from the chomping crawlers.

"No, no, no stop." She pleas with the window, as the pressure from both sides cause its integrity to slowly fail, until ultimately shattering it into a million tiny pieces.

Bodies spill out backwards into the awaiting crowd of chomping dead. Even the few that catch their balance are either pushed out by the force of those struggling inside or ripped out by the flesh-cravers outside as victims are passed back through the lifeless crowd like some cannibalistic concert stunt.

On the tarmac, out in the distance, stands two figures. It's the newly transformed German scientist overlooking his infections wrath and his loyal Japanese General that released him from the train.

They're observing the mayhem as it takes place. Both have their arms folded and the German is stroking his chin with the look of stone on his gray face.

"Two…planes…escaped." The General reports.

"Don't worry. The military and air traffic are destroyed." The scientist states in his German accent, "Now, send them to block the highways."

"Total containment."

"Yes. Then begin recruiting." The scientist says coldly before turning and walking away.

A grin comes over the twisted General's face as he obviously enjoys his job. He looks back at the chaos with pride and then mumbles to himself in his own heavy accent, "Yes, sir."

In the sky, flight 187 has just made its way over the Las Vegas Strip. The older distinguished looking pilot, with gray at the temples, tries desperately to make contact with the ground.

"Tower, this is flight 187. Come in tower. We're not receiving any incoming information or communications from you. I don't know if it's an error on our side or yours, over."

"I saw some sort of blast on the ground as we took off. It must have knocked out their communications." The young co-pilot mentions.

A slap at the cockpit door is slow and persistent.

"See who that is. I'm going to keep trying them."

The young co-pilot unbuckles himself and stands up to release the handle on the door. A strong push comes from the other side, as soon as the latch is freed. This sudden rush knocks the unsuspecting co-pilot back on his heels and into the back of the pilot.

The moans of lip-less flight attendant's and their scratching outstretched, bloodied limbs and exposed bone digits barge their way through the single entrance.

Somehow the intercom button is hit in the struggle and without censor the pilot's dire screams are broadcast throughout the entire plane.

The muffled battle instantly causes the passengers to panic as the plane begins to shake and plummet. Oxygen masks drop from the ceiling as trays and carts spill debris everywhere. The downward tilt of the plane is so sharp that it only takes a few moments before it bursts through the side of one of the city's unsuspecting mega resorts.

The impact causes an explosion that sends flames shooting up and out of the Las Vegas landmark with such fury that it consumes a majority of the casino and parts of the adjacent properties in seconds.

CHAPTER FIFTEEN

"This just in, it seems that unprecedented events are taking place in Las Vegas, Nevada. Initial reports are that some sort of terrorist attack has taken place and as a result it has completely cut off communications with both Nellis Air Force Base and the McCarran International Airport. A confidential military source reports, no distress calls have been received from either the base or the airport before they went black. All other attempts to make contact with the city have gone unanswered." Reports the on-air anchorman, who pauses to let someone off-camera whispering into his ear, "This just in, it seems we have aerial photographs that might show us what is happening on the ground. We'd like to warn you, these images might be graphic."

Video images play out on the broadcast. They start with the entire city landscape, as seen from outer space, and zoom in on the base down to the street level.

The bones of the devoured soldiers lie strewn about the road along with their torn uniforms and dried blood. Amongst them are less destroyed bodies that lie contorted in the gutters. Suddenly movement comes from one of the bodies, then another. Soon the bodies begin to twitch and raise as one position its arm underneath itself, just enough to lift its body to its feet. This bizarre scene is followed by another and another who all begin to rise to their feet.

"Are those dead bodies getting up?" The confused anchor asks his producer.

"What the hell is going on?" He continues until it's brought to his attention again that he's live-on-the-air.

"Ah-hem, sorry folks." The anchor says gathering himself, "It seems other videos of similar events happening all throughout the tourist capital are hitting the web and going viral."

UNDISCLOSED LOCATION
U.S.A.

The interior of the military planning room is filled with the nation's political and military leaders. The heated, unorganized discussions of what to do first are being shouted out across a big round table.

Collages of the latest streaming videos play out on the screen-filled wall behind them.

A large man, in a dark blue suit, and a notable scar across his forehead slams his fist into the table causing a boom that quiets the room.

"Quiet!" He pauses, "We know what this is. We've seen it infecting facilities all over the globe. Just never on this scale. We know this attack was planned in answer to our participation in this man's project."

The man pushes a button and the screens change to feature a younger, healthier looking photo of the German scientist.

"Hans Essex, a second generation Nazi scientist whose father was responsible for thousands of helpless deaths in World War II. Hans spoke out against these acts and instead, offered his father's life work up as a gesture to help as many as he could. A little more than a year ago, he called a secret meeting in Hawaii and offered a select few nations, samples and data for a new cure-all formula. He was afraid he wouldn't live long enough to see it completed. Unfortunately, the failed attempts to fix the formula spawned a variety of new reactions that resulted in these things we're seeing all over Vegas."

"So it's biological?" Someone asks.

"Yes, and highly contagious." The man replies.

Another military man on the other side of the table speaks up, "We can't send any more of our boys in their after what happened at Nellis. We need to send an inbound strike to destroy it all from the sky."

"What do you mean? Nuke a city of millions, that's full of tourists from all over the world? Forget it! The international ramifications are immeasurable and the president won't sign off on it." The president's personal adviser chimes in, "Especially with it being an election year."

A soldier whispers into the ear of the large man in the blue suit. The man nods, and presses another button to change the screens, yet again.

"The families, protestors, politicians, and corporations who own everything in Vegas are refusing to support any kind of mass scale cleansing of this situation and the military doesn't want to risk a mass insurgence of soldiers on the ground to fight against something with these kinds of numbers and results."

"So, what do we do?"

"Well, watch this..."

The screen goes black and then a quick flash of a shaky cam on the street plays; it cuts out for a half a second before returning to reveal someone is filming on the streets of Las Vegas.

They seem to be in front of one of the resorts, as the automated water show is going off in the background. The camera is focused down the strip at an approaching mass of undead and sees that they are actually chasing a couple dozen tourists up the street.

As the herd of zombie dead hit the corner, they are attacked by what looks like a larger version of one of their own. It's the monstrous Michael, charging to put separating between the dead and their living victims.

The cameraman focuses and zooms in just in time to see Michael swipe the head completely off the shoulders of a wild runner. Then, as a hoard of crawlers surround him he begins pulling arms and legs off, one right after another, until he is left standing in the center of a pile of bodies holding an arm he broke off at the elbow. From behind, a newly converted Elvis impersonator attempts to pounce on Michael's back, only to be met with the severed forearm being shoved completely through his skull.

From the overhead walkway, an armed Alexis repels down followed by her Uncle Jason, Ivan, the talker Michael spared in Kingman, and the rest of his undead converts.

They immediately begin their own bloody assault on the

enemy regiment while pushing forward.

Michael, covered in blood and guts, turns to the people now cowering with the cameraman.

"Stay with us. We're on your side." He says eerily before returning to the fight.

The cameraman confirms it's alright and leads the tourists out behind the crew.

Back in the war room, the men are silent.

They turn and wait for the large man, who's obviously in charge, to speak.

"Fight death with the dead. I like that. Even if they lose someone, they're already dead, so who cares?"

Now, focused back on the screen and back to the action live.

Moving slowly down the strip the assault crew is spread out in a line. They're destroying dead like lawnmowers tearing over turf. Michael's army of immune females and converted dead-head's continue amassing uninfected tourists along the way.

Ivan stands by Michael's side with Jason on the other. They form a sort of triangle in the middle of the street that allows them to cover each direction. The pop of machine gun fire, mixed with the grunts of skull crushing swings, surrounds them.

Alexis is off to the side and accompanied by two others.

She shoots a repulsively fat crawler in its head point blank, right before her partner slashes its decrepit body in half with a single swing of his sword. As its pieces flop to the ground she notices in the distance, Sam pulling the head off a ravenous former cop. He notices her giving him a look, and smiles a gray, bloody smile before they both return to the battle.

CHAPTER SIXTEEN

The battles are now being fought in rapidly decaying casinos, the sprawling Vegas suburbs, and even underground in the city's massive sewer tunnel system.

Needless to say, nowhere is safe.

As the last of the current undead bodies fall, Ivan drops a severed head into the wet gutter. Without flinching, Michael and Jason stand strong as an old military truck races to a screeching stop inches from them.

Inside, a pregnant Cindy sits behind the wheel with great confidence in her eyes. Even though she should only be a few months along, her belly seems to show something different.

Addy's in the passenger seat and a smile comes over her face when she sees her dad and sister alive. In the bed of the truck, stands the monstrous looking Al. His paws poised up on the wheel hump, as he growls out in baritone at the dead lifeless bodies strewn about. He jumps down out of the truck and begins sniffing around. His irregular huffing leads him off to make the rounds through the bodies.

He's looking for any threats.

The rumbling of a nearby manhole cover catches his attention. In anticipation, a stream of thick drool begins falling from his fangs.

"What is it boy?" Addy asks looking in the direction Al's now creeping.

"I know that look." Jason says pointing his guns at the manhole cover, "He smells trouble."

This grabs the attention of the others who begin to circle around.

Another abrupt rumble of the lid startles Addy causing her to yelp. A serious Michael, not interested in playing any games, kneels down in front of the lid.

"Some of them must have wandered down into the sewer. Just be ready when I pop the lid."

He grabs the lip of the lid and tugs on it, but it doesn't come completely up. He tries again, but now notices a clumpy weld holding part of it in place.

"What's that hiss sound?" Jason asks.

"It's coming from down here?" Michael adds as smoke is now seeping through the holes of the lid.

"Dynamite. It's a burning fuse!"

"Get back!"

The crew dives out of the way just as the lid blows ten feet into the air, landing hard and spinning just a few feet away.

From inside the dark hole peaks out a leather-bound head wearing dirty swim goggles and a nose plug. Its eyes fixated on Michael, Ivan, and the rest of the converted.

If you weren't aware, you wouldn't know the difference between them and the other dead, so there's no motion at first.

Then, the tip of a machine gun slowly appears from the hole. At the same time, more voices are heard mumbling underground.

Before the masked man can take aim, Michael snatches him and the gun up and out of the hole in a single move. He hands the gun off and pulls the mask off to reveal a man in his mid-twenties.

"What the hell are you doing down there?" Michael asks.

"You talk?" He responds shocked at the thought.

"I feel like saying something sarcastic." Michael snarks.

"We're surviving, that's what we're doing down there. Surviving your kind!" The man says trying to struggle free before going limp, "Hey, how can you talk?"

Michael has to take a second to remember how he appears before responding.

"I'm not like them." He says setting the man down.

"So, you don't feed?"

"No, not like them. I don't have the same hunger." Michael answers.

"How many people do you have down there?" Jason asks peeking over the edge.

"I'm not sure, quite a few? But we're growing by the day."

"Yeah, us too." Jason adds backing up.

"You're working with them?" The man asks Jason when he notices the other humans standing around.

"Who's in charge, you?" Ivan asks in his accent.

"That's complicated, dead man. I guess it depends on who you ask..."

Suddenly, a single shot rings out from behind them. The bullet misses its target and ricochets off the ground. Then, before anyone can react, another shot reigns out ripping completely through Ivan's shoulder and lodging itself into Michael's.

"What the hell?" Michael exclaims swatting at the wound like he'd been bit by a bug.

The man drops back down into the sewer hole where he disappears in the dark.

Turning to face their attacker, the crew instantly prepares to kill whatever it is. Only to their surprise it's not what they expect, instead it's a little old lady with a semi-automatic hunting rifle.

She's staring them all down without a flinch.

Behind her stands a growing group of soccer moms, fast food workers, and other everyday people. All armed with whatever everyday items they could find.

CHAPTER SEVENTEEN

From every underground nook and hole pours out an ever growing mass that is now lining up behind the grandmother figure.

It's an endless stream of these surprisingly normal looking everyday citizens. They're from all walks of life and look worn and dirty, but serious. Amongst the crowd, is the young mother from the airport. She's without her son and paying extra attention to Addy who is right around the age of her son.

Her eyes begin to well up.

Al growls at their aggressive display, even causing their front line to take a step back.

"Al! Get over here boy!" The monstrous Michael calls out.

They cower back even further at the sight of him and his approaching dead soldiers. The looks in their eyes are unsure of what to do, fight or flea. Then, Michael steps out in front of his men to get a feel of this new challenge.

"We're not the enemy." Michael says putting his palm in the air, "We came here to help."

The elderly leader lowers her weapon and takes a step forward.

"I don't know what you are, but you look like one of those things that killed my son and destroyed my life, the same kind of dead thing that came to this city with the sole mission of turning all of us into one of those dead things, like you."

By this time, the crowd behind her has begun to nod their heads to show that they agree with her. Some even begin shaking their fists as they mumble along with her. For the most part, they seem to be getting some satisfaction that they're finally being heard.

"I know how you feel, even more so. They destroyed our whole town and killed almost everyone we knew. They turned the rest of us into what stands here. My brother-in-law is a chemist and he's come up with a vaccine and can use it to immunize the females and give the men, if attacked, the ability to remain in control of their minds." Michael looks down at his massive gray hands, "Our bodies are another story."

"So, we should just trust you?"

"Yes. We could use your knowledge of the city's terrain and resources to ramp up our efforts. Plus, we can offer some protection and we still have enough of the serum to treat most, if not all of you."

"Keep your poison and use it on those more desperate."

The docile, yet menacing looking, Al stands next to Addy wagging his tail. He again catches the eye of the staring woman.

"We haven't seen any other animals survive the infection. They get bit and eventually just die from the poisoning." The elder comments.

"We treated him too." Michael answers scratching Al's head as Addy hugs his neck, "She loves him so much I couldn't let him die… completely."

"So, you can treat anyone?"

"In theory, yes." Jason answers.

The woman pauses, as if she's thinking about someone in particular.

"Alright everybody, gather up those survivors over there and let's get back underground before it gets dark."

"So that's it? No partnership, no sticking together?" Michael asks confused that his offers been shot down, "We can fight this thing head on, with greater odds of success if we have greater numbers."

She responds bluntly, "Your women can come with us if they want. But as far as us 'teaming up' to fight these things, we're not at that stage yet. We're out here looking for our friends and families. If we run into something, well, that's different. But we're not picking any fights."

Ivan leans in sideways to get close enough to Michael's ear to whisper, "Just let them go. It's just more people we'd have to watch over."

"That's the point." Michael says without making eye contact with him, "What if we agree to help?" Michael directs back at her as she's walking away.

"We're successful because we're under the radar. You guys

are all over the place. I'm sorry, it may be short-sided of me, but we're going to stick with what works."

"I'm not going to beg." Michael tries to reason, "It's just with so many people, hiding in so many places, they can only remain hidden for so long."

She turns with a smile on her face.

"So much wisdom coming out of that battle worn face, thank you sir, but still, we'll pass. I'm sure we'll cross paths again. Like you said, there are only so many places to go in this city."

Michael shakes his head and the people slowly return to their underground sanctuary taking several of the rescued tourists with them.

The lonely, childless woman continues to stare, as she starts down the manhole. She takes another long look at Addy and sighs before disappearing.

CHAPTER EIGHTEEN

"She has a point." Michael says barely audible and leaning back to sit on the hood of an old Buick, "We need to remember we were human."

The night is surprisingly dark, especially since the neon glow of the strip isn't what it used to be. The dwindling numbers of Michael's dead enforcers has taken its toll on all of them. The looks on their faces and the way their heads hang indicate that this number is larger than they had expected. As a matter of fact, of the several dozen that came with them, only a few dozen remain. Of those, several are healing and the unconverted are exhausted.

The 50 gallon drum that they've filled with debris and set on fire glows just enough to warm, but not enough to draw attention.

Alexis and Addy are lying in the bed of the truck, next to each other.

"Tomorrow we'll find a quiet cul-de-sac to sleep in, maybe an empty house with a real bed and clean clothes."

"Yeah, maybe we'll be able to rescue some abandoned pets too."

"Pets? Even with all that's going on you're still thinking about animals?"

"Yeah, so? Who else is thinking about them?"

"You're so weird." Alexis adds rolling over.

The next day, as the sun is at its highest and the heat is dry and unbearable, the crew has begun to go door-to-door in one of the older historic neighborhoods.

Single, intermittent shots ring out here and there as straggling undead emerge from the aftermath of the initial onslaught tearing through before quickly moving on.

"Do you hear that?" Alexis asks the others she's patrolling with, "It came from over here?"

"I didn't hear anything? Did you?" One asks the other.

"No." They reply.

Regardless, Alexis makes her way up the arched driveway and through the small gate that leads to the front door. Through the glass accented door, she hears what sounds like a baby saying, "Mommy."

Her heart starts pumping faster when she hears the same little voice now crying. She shoots the door knob and pushes her way into the house.

Inside, she finds the home has been thrashed. Furniture has been overturned and blood splattered on the walls.

As she tries to follow where the sounds is coming from, she becomes visibly emotional. Her fear causes her to dart from room to room, until she busts into the master bedroom.

Inside, she finds a trail of blood leading from the closet to the bathroom. As she takes her first step, she can see movement in the reflection of the mirrored closet door. Not being cautious, and remaining focused on her target, she steps towards the movement, accidentally stepping on something hard that causes her to pull up quickly.

"Mommy. Whaa." A doll yelps from under her feet.

The sound causes the runner in the bathroom to look up and turn to face the sound. A twitch of its head and it's up from its current meal and in the doorway staring Alexis up and down.

Something's different. The normally blurry-fast beast seems to be slower in Alexis' eyes.

As it attacks, she dodges its jaws clutches with ease. Even as it spins around for a follow up lunge, she seems to be one step ahead of it as she thrusts her knife deep into its head. It drops motionless. She breaks down in tears of relief as she looks over at the doll.

A moment later she emerges from the house covered in blood splatter. Her eyes are smeared black with streaks of mascara running down her cheeks.

As the sun hits her face, she squints and sees Sam off in the distance. A smile fills her face as she sees her first love, not as a dead boy, but as the boy who tried too hard to be cool.

She has that look on her face that tells anyone paying attention that she still likes him, even after all this..

Ivan sees Alexis' emotional glare and smacks Sam on the back of the head before pointing her out to him from across the lawn.

He quickly looks up through his jaundiced eyes and sees Alexis' emotional face staring at him. He cracks a thin smile back at her.

She instantly drops her head and puts on a shy act that causes her to quickly turn and walk away.

CHAPTER NINETEEN

"Do you think we're alright wandering this far into the neighborhood, babe?" Cindy asks a very serious Jason.

"We should be fine. I just know I saw a few houses with swing sets over this way." He says as he reaches to pull himself up to look over a brick wall, "This is the one, come on."

The two make their way around to the front of the house.

"They definitely had kids." Cindy says peeking through the front window, "There are toys everywhere."

Jason kicks in the front door. Then turns to see his pregnant wife holding her stomach as if she's reminiscent of the way it could be.

"Come on babe. Let's see what baby stuff we can salvage."

"Yeah, alright, I'm ready." She says snapping back to reality. Then, just as she is about to step through the door, she stops to feel the door frame and takes in the home.

"No! Stop! Leave me alone!" the struggling plea comes from an unknown source somewhere nearby, maybe across the street.

A puzzled look comes over Cindy's face as she seems to recognize the voice crying out.

"Babe! There's trouble!" She says turning from the house

and rushing towards the voice.

Jason follows only a few steps behind her. When she reaches the side gate of the house, they hear more commotion coming from the backyard.

"No, no, no." The male voice cries out again.

"Move babe." Jason tells Cindy so he can force the gate open.

Once in the backyard, the scene is playing out before them. An older man is in the shallow end of the oblong swimming pool, fighting off a recently turned younger man. He's holding him off with the pole from the leaf skimmer.

The thrashing and splashing around in the water leaves visibility limited for Jason as he takes aim for the attackers head.

Then, just as the dead lunges teeth first for the old man, the water settles enough to allow Jason a clean head shot. It drops the apparently nude beast face first into the water. The wound rapidly seeps into the water acting like a disgustingly deadly tea bag that turns the water a brownish red.

It's then that Cindy remembers where she heard that voice. It's the older guy she met at the airport. The one she met while waiting for her brother to arrive. Which means the body floating face down in the pool was his younger boyfriend.

"Are you alright?" Cindy asks helping the shocked man out of the pool.

"No, I don't think I am." He says glancing back at the floating body, then back up at her, "It's you. From the..."

"Yes." Cindy stops him mid-sentence with a hug.

Jason sighs with a sense of relief that the situation didn't go any further.

In that moment, an angry runner bolts from the house, smashing into the old man and plowing Cindy to the ground. Her head bounces off the concrete deck and the impact and weight of the man snaps her back.

Rebounding in a single move, the speedy demon lunges at its next target with intent. Jason's hit in the chest and the momentum forces him and his attacker into the bloodied pool.

Underwater the runners speed is nullified and Jason is able to avoid its initial strikes. Then, pulling the long serrated hunting knife from his belt, he takes aim at the runners' skull as it's wrestling to take a chunk out of one of his legs. As he begins to thrust at the undead, it suddenly pushes off the pools floor and blasts up towards Jason's face. Before he can get the knife positioned for the kill, the dead sinks his lipless teeth into Jason's upper chest. He lets out a bubbly cry as he struggles to break the grasp of the thing.

A tug on Jason's hand catches him off guard as his knife is ripped from his hand leaving him defenseless. Then, a quick jarring of the beast head causes it to go limp and release its hold. At the other end of the knife is the shaking old man. He quickly releases his hold of the blade that's now left sticking out of attackers' skull.

He pulls back cringing as Jason pulls himself to the pools steps to rest.

"He was one of our friends. He came over to wait out the events, after the club he was at was attacked. I didn't know he was bit."

Cindy comes to, moaning in pain. Jason crawls over to be closer to her leaving a blood trail behind him.

The old man rushes to her side putting a towel under her head.

"Is she alright?" Jason asks, "Uh, I'm sorry I don't know your name?"

"Bobby, or Bob I'm a doctor. She might have a concussion and her back might have some damage from the impact."

"How does she know you?"

"We met at the airport." He says pausing again to look at the dead bodies in the pool, "She's much further along looking than she should be. What have the doctors said?"

"This all happened so fast, she hasn't seen one yet."

"Pick her up carefully and bring her inside. I have my *house call bag* in my study."

Inside, Jason lies her down on the couch while Dr. Bob goes to retrieve his bag. Cindy comes to laughing in pain when she sees the portrait of Liberace over the fireplace.

The home is all white on white, and very plush. This makes the recent activity and blood drops stand out even more.

When the doctor returns he pulls a stethoscope and portable ultrasound tool from his bag. He begins his examination asking things like, "Does it hurt here or here?" A few minutes pass and he pulls the scope from his ears.

"We'll, first thing you appear to be closer to thirty-five weeks pregnant than you are to eight or ten? Also, the impact has caused trauma to the embryonic sack. I believe one of your ribs may have fractured and punctured it." He pauses for a second, "Plus, there's not just one heart beat in there. It sounds like twins and I'm afraid one of them might be hurt because the heart rates aren't even and one is becoming faint."

"So, what can we do?" Jason asks as Cindy is now freaking out and breathing heavy.

"If we were in the hospital, I'd say let's operate, and unfortunately, I think we're going to have to anyway."

Just then, the doctor sees the gash on the back of Cindy's sideways turned head. It begins to quickly close on its own.

"What the hell?"

"What doc?" Jason asks.

"The wound on her neck is just closing up on its own."

"Yeah, she's special. She's been immunized to the infection and this advanced healing is one of the side effects. But I've only been able to get it to work like this well for females."

"That might explain the rapid pregnancy and might be just what she's going to need to survive this delivery."

"I agree. I'm going to run and grab the others before they go looking for us in the wrong direction."

"Alright, I'll get ready for the babies." Bobby says returning to his study.

"I'll be right back, babe." Jason says kissing Cindy's forehead before rushing off.

CHAPTER TWENTY

The flow of salty sweat begins to sting in his eyes, as Jason races back to the others. He cuts under a low hanging tree and across a few yards until he rounds the final corner.

Off in the distance, he can see groups going in and out of houses and piling supplies on the curb. He tries to cry out, but his throat is too dry.

Unusually dry.

He takes only a few more steps before the pain in his chest shoots through his body causing his legs to give out.

As he attempts to crawl forward, the painful protrusion of his transforming veins that are now spidering through his flesh show to be too much. His body's reaction causes him to fall out unconscious.

Up the street, Addy sees her uncle collapse to his knees and yells out. Al sniffs the air and barks out gaining the attention of the others who rush over to him. His twitching body appears to be fighting the infection in a whole new way not seen before.

Michael bends down and picks Jason up to carry him back to the truck.

"The inoculation must be fighting the serum and his body is stuck in the middle. Where's Cindy?" Michael asks before yelling out, "Hey! Has anyone seen my sister?"

A couple of those around him shake their heads.

"Find her; she's got to be somewhere and she's probably in trouble."

Meanwhile, Bobby has begun the operation to deliver the babies. He injects Cindy with something to minimize what he assumes is pain. Her writhing dulls down as the doctor wipes down her lower abdomen with iodine before slicing into her to perform the caesarian.

"Alright now, just try to relax the best you can." Bobby calmly instructs.

"Where's Jason?" Cindy asks in her groggy state.

"He went to get the others. Now relax, we have to get started." He says putting a moist cloth on her forehead.

A bang from the front of the house echoes down the hall. This causes Bobby to turn his head unsure of what to expect. He gets up and walks away from the table to peak out through the crack in the door to see what he's dealing with. He gets an obstructed view of what is obvious a dead man.

Panic comes over his eyes knowing they are vulnerable and that he only has a set window in time to deliver the babies before the injuries become too much a factor and it risks the unborn lives.

As he tries to shut the door, a greenish-gray, vein riddled hand stops it about an inch from being sealed.

The strength of the beast is firm as it presses open the

door. This causes the doctor to slide then fall back in fear.

Then, as the door swings open completely, Bobby reaches for a ceramic dog statue to mount his defense.

"Sam?" Cindy says half out of it.

This baffles the doctor.

"Yeah, it's me. We've been looking for you. What happened?"

Bobby sets the figurine down confused.

"Where's Jason?" She asks again.

"He's been hurt. But the serum seems to be helping. I'm going to get the others. Will you be alright?" Sam asks.

"Yes, Bobby is my friend," she says pointing to the doctor like a drunken woman, "He's fabulous and gay."

"I am." He says with a crooked smile and a shrug, "But I have to get started if I'm going to save them." Bobby says with tiny 'hello' wave.

Several minutes later, outside the home, Sam returns with everybody.

Inside, the doctor has pulled the first child out and is about to set her down in her mother's arms. As he reaches in to pull out the second baby, Michael's massive frame comes barging in through the door.

Bobby jumps back startled.

Michael's rendered motionless when he sees the activities.

Bobby creeps back over to Cindy where he cautiously begins to pull the second baby out. As he grabs hold of the feet he starts to pull. The sight of its dark gray flesh has Bobby giving Michael a double take. He continues to pull the baby from the womb, only to reveal that it's some sort of new mutation.

As Bobby clears its little throat, it doesn't begin to cry. Instead, it lets out an eerie moan. Michael's eyes widen as the doctor wraps it in a blanket, unsure if he should hand it to Cindy.

"Let me see doc. Is it another girl?" Cindy asks with here eye's half shut.

"No, it's a boy." He replies.

"He looks like his uncle." Michael says softly with sarcasm in his tone, "You okay sis?"

"Where's Jason?"

"He was bit. It looks like he's reacting differently. He was inoculated before the infection, so I'm not sure how long it'll take. But, he's safe in the truck." He answers her.

"This serum is why you're sort of normal and can talk?" Bobby asks.

"Yes." Michael says as he finally takes the baby boy from the doctor and he hugs it to his shoulder.

"Rowan and Riot." Cindy states blankly before passing out.

Bobby begins to stitch Cindy up, while baby Rowan is passed on to Alexis, who's crept into the room.

"I guess that makes you Riot?" Michael says softly to the baby beast in his hands, "Sort of a fitting name for such a handsome guy."

Suddenly, behind each stitch, Cindy's wounds begin to heal right before the doctors eyes.

"Remarkable." He says in amazement.

Outside, the afternoon has begun to turn to night again and the crew of misfits has gathered on the doctor's front lawn. Jason lies shivering in the back of the truck, pale and thin skinned in appearance. His veins lifting slowly, but it's nothing like the others and that gives hope.

What's left of the converted dead are sprawled across the lawn sprinkled throughout in the crowd are the unconverted fighters. Everyone seems to be enjoying this moment of peace while they wait for Cindy and the babies to emerge.

When the door opens, Alexis steps out holding baby Rowan and those crowded in the yard shift their attention instantly to them. As she walks out to let them see the newest addition to their clan, the emotional human side of the would-be rotting warriors has a second to surface.

This sight momentarily takes their minds far from battle.

Then, as if it was timed, in the distance a large roaming group of dead jump the fences at the end of the block. They look as if they used to be some sort of football team, stained from head to toe with mud and blood. They seem to smell the groups pink flesh and are ready to feast.

The first runner breaks through the crowd without resistance. It's bloody, drooling teeth targeting baby Rowan like she's some sort of delicacy. But, just as the killer pounces, Sam jumps in the way, shoulder first, and drives the unsuspecting attacker to the ground.

Alexis pulls the baby back into her chest and spins to put her back to the fight while the rest of the bodies clash in an impromptu battle. But these dead are athletic and stronger than most and the fight gets ugly.

Ivan is split between fighting what use to be the city's all-conference nose tackle and one of the state's heavyweight class wrestling champions. One hits him low, while the other goes high. He's knocked to the ground hard.

While down, he sees the woman from the earlier confrontation with the underground militia in the gutter, eyeballing Addy. Unfortunately, he doesn't have time to worry and is forced to keep fighting as he's drug back by his ankles.

On the other side of the street, Addy is left alone hiding behind a large utility box after Al has raced down the center of the street after one of the faster attackers.

Michael comes out of the house to find the havoc in full swing. He rushes out to join the fight by crushing through the closest enemies head before taking any and every one on.

The sun sets before it's over. The battle was bloody, but Michael's fighters are the victors.

On the sidewalk, next to the utility box, the sewer lid has been lifted up and out of its home.

Al sniffs around, whining in search of something. Michael notices him and his strange behavior and then he notices what's missing.

"Addy? Where's Addy?"

Al stops and sniffs down into the hole.

CHAPTER TWENTY-ONE

Deep down in the darkness of the Las Vegas sewer system, Michael and Ivan are searching for Addy. They crawl through tunnels, down shafts, and wade through waste. The smell would be unbearable, if the two hadn't smelled worst coming out of their own bodies.

"This way." Ivan says confidently stepping up onto a short ladder that leads to an elevated shaft.

By now the twists and turns have lead the two so far away from their point of origin, that the ability to backtrack has long since passed.

"Are you sure they would've come this way?" Michael asks as he looks down at the waste he's sloshing through.

"Yeah, I can smell them, up here."

The two climb up a long shaft where at the top, Ivan lifts the heavy cover up and out of the way. He climbs out ahead leaving Michael a few steps behind.

When Michael reaches the top of the hole he's smashed in the face with the manhole cover which forces him to drop back down into the shaft.

He awakes to the sound of someone being smacked that's echoing down the empty hall. Michael's lethargic eyes begin to crack open, just as a third smack approaches his cheek. Even with his mind still fuzzy, and unaware of his surroundings, he's able to pull back out of the way, causing the strike to whiff past his face.

He turns his head from side-to-side trying to find Ivan. He's nowhere in the room. When he tries to stands up, several arms reach out on each side of him. They pull him firmly back down.

"I get it. I've killed your killers so now you want a piece of me in revenge." Michael says motioning with his hands.

An unfamiliar voice, with a heavy accent, similar to Ivan's, begins to rant.

"Huh, you seem very confident for such a bug, you and your little band of dead. I want you to suffer and I want the same world that's rooting for you, to see you die on the inside." He says jabbing his finger into Michael's chest, "Not just for the interference, but for your bold defiance to adversity. For this, I will be the one to kill their only chance at a hero."

As he finishes, he turns and triggers the wall of curtains that surround them to move. They open revealing that they're actually sitting over 1,100 feet in the air, on top of the tallest hotel in the city.

Hans steps in front of the clear, panoramic view to gaze out on the mess he's created. He makes a single hand motion and his thugs begin to pound on Michael.

CHAPTER TWENTY-TWO

"What are you doing? Let me go." Addy says struggling to free her wrist from the woman's surprisingly strong grip.

"I can't let you be in that kind of danger anymore. Little kids and those things aren't supposed to be that close. They'll turn on you."

"They're my family and friends?"

"That doesn't matter. They'll turn and you're such an easy target. I'm only trying to save you."

Confused as she's being drug through the dark tunnel, Addy looks behind her and all around. She's trying to find an out or some sign of daylight.

Meanwhile, on the surface AI has left the others to search on his own. He's following his instincts to find Addy.

He seems to be on a determined path.

Back down below, the two have stepped into a wider, box-shaped room with vents for a roof. These openings let the daylight through. A dull colored iron ladder leads up to the surface.

"The others will protect you from those things. You'll be safe with us, come on." The woman says dragging Addy up the ladder with her.

"I don't need protection. I was safe until you stole me." She says pulling back.

"I'm sorry." The woman says softly as she begins to breakdown emotionally.

Addy sees the tears and begins to feel compassion.

"I lost my son during the airport attack and I've just been so...I don't know."

"Just take me back."

The woman ignores her and continues up the ladder. Addy struggles with her, but eventually follows her up.

When they reach the top, the woman pushes the grate up and out of the way. She lifts herself out and helps Addy up.

As soon as the woman bends to dust herself off, she hears a familiar deep growl approaching her from behind. Her eyes widen as she's overcome with fear.

She slowly turns to face a toothy Al.

His snarl and grotesque appearance is enough to scare any regular person. But, instead of cowering, the woman slowly reaches for something in her waist. Her slow reach reveals she has a hidden chrome revolver. As she grips the handle, the gleam of the sun catches Addy's eye.

She drops her backpack preparing for the altercation.

"No! Don't!" She yells diving for the woman's arms. Then, Al snaps his jaw at the woman as she accidentally lets off a shot into the air. Al's momentum forces her back and his paws pin her on her back as Addy gets the gun.

"Come on boy!" Addy says backing away from the woman with the gun in her hand, "Don't you follow us. I am sorry about your son, but I'm not just some replacement. I have a family."

Addy grabs her pack and the two back off, keeping an eye on the now weeping woman.

Down the street and far enough away to feel safe, Addy takes a moment to assess the situation. She realizes that they'll have to cross the dangerous Vegas Strip to get back to the family. But, every time they have been on the strip before, they were in some sort of fight only now they're alone.

She jumps up into the back of an abandon 4X4. Al circles around her, keeping guard. Looking out from her elevated position, she can see the strip and the huge valley behind it. Her concern shows on her little face.

"I don't know buddy? This place is a lot bigger than Kingman. I think we're lost."

Al looks up and whimpers.

As they approach the mammoth casinos, her worst fears are roaming free around what's left of the neon blinking streets. Before they're discovered, she ducks down into a service entrance behind one of the bigger buildings.

"Maybe we can cut through the casino?" She says leading Al into the building.

Inside, the eerie empty back halls are littered with racks of disgusting dishes, stacks of folded tables, and endless rows of abandoned porter carts. Chaotic proof of how fast daily life really did just halt.

Making her way through the winding, behind-the-scene corridors, Addy is cautious with every new step and Al remains right next to her.

"Whew, what's that smell?" Addy says pulling her shirt up over her nose.

In an attempt to find its source, she opens a black and silver door labeled 'Habitat'. The stench is intensified, as she steps through with caution.

Inside, she finds a long, dimly lit hallway with large Plexiglas windows. The first window is blood stained and all she can make out is the body of one of the trainers lying face down. They look as if they've been torn apart after being infected.

Behind the second window, a large Bengal tiger is prowling around in the back of the habitat. Its lips are gray and its eyes are blood shot. Its mouth is dripping an excessive amount of drool and blood.

Further down the hall she finds a mature female lion and an angry white tiger are both in similar condition and both with blood stained jowls. She steps in to pay closer attention, only to notice that they all seem to be especially irritated.

An even closer inspection reveals the mangled dead bodies of even more trainers, all of which seemed to have been infected and now the beasts are infected as well.

She can see the pain in their faces.

"I can't leave them like this." She says to Al who replies with an uncertain growl.

She pulls the bag from her shoulder and unzips it. Inside it's not filled with the typical "little girl" swag, instead it's filled with doses of her uncle's serum. Now with an even more determined look in her eyes, she pulls the first pre-filled injector from the bag and prepares to enter the white tiger's lair.

Al rubs against her requesting a farewell stroke. She smiles and rustles the hair on his head. He gives her a slobbery kiss on the mouth that leaves her dripping. She instantly tries wiping it clean with her empty hand but it's too much.

"You know you have to stay here so you don't rile each other up just yet." Addy says to Al.

As the door creeps open, the stench of human flesh and beast waste fills her nostrils. The beautiful, but crazed beast sits pulled back into the corner confused. As she creeps up to him, she slowly shows him her palms before stopping several feet away.

"Hey, don't be scared. I'm here to help. I have something to help you feel better." She says extending her empty, yet still slobbery hand.

The lioness's growl is already deeper than Al's monstrous moan. As it sniffs out at her, she smiles and doesn't move. This confidence conveys something to the animal and it slowly creeps towards her still sniffing the air.

As it reaches her, she pets it softly for a moment before injecting the serum into a section of its loose skin.

"Okay, Lea, that's what I'm going to call you, I'm going to give you a minute until you feel better." She says calmly backing out of the habitat.

Outside, she rushes to the glass to keep an eye on her new friend. The beast circles and circles until it collapses in the fetal position. The change happens quickly, as the already large animal seems to swell several inches in each direction. Until upon completion, it growls out like thunder that rattles the walls.

Stepping out of the casino with a smug confidence, Addy stands tall with Al by her side. The new motion of the door slamming shut and clamping behind her, turns the heads of several of the roaming dead in the street. They're attention is now focused, as the sound draws them to her.

She doesn't budge.

Just as the first crawler gets within a few feet from her, Al begins to growl and the glass doors behind her are shattered out into a million pieces. The converted white tiger's thick paws land with a thud on the solid concrete. It's followed closely by the other two converted cats.

In only a single step of the approaching dead's, the three beasts and Al pounce with an unprecedented level of protection, devouring and decapitating everything that dared to approach.

The sense of safety, mixed with pride, causes Addy's eyes

to well up.

CHAPTER TWENTY-THREE

"Uh? Ugh." Jason shivers and cringes in pain lying in a ball on Bobby's couch.

Cindy is in the bedroom nursing Rowan while Riot lies on the bed with a bottle propped in his mouth. Michael's backpack sits on the end of the bed.

Bobby enters the bedroom carrying a bowl of soup for Cindy.

"Hey, momma, how are you and the miracle twins doing?" He asks.

"Alright. I've bonded with this one, but he sort of scares me." She says with concern on her face.

"He's your child. He won't hurt you. He hasn't learned those behaviors yet."

Cindy nods, "How's Jason?"

"He's in pain. But, he hasn't changed yet. He's still...him? It's like he's stuck in-between. I'm not really sure how long his body can take the trauma and I'm not sure what to do in this situation."

"He would probably give himself more serum."

"If we only had more." Bobby replies.

"We do." Cindy says using her foot to kick the backpack.

Bobby walks over and opens the pack revealing the small canister of serum and a few prepared doses. He grabs a dose and heads back out of the room. Cindy follows.

Outside, Sam is sitting on the porch alone staring at the ground. Alexis sits down next to him and gives him a nudge.

"Hey." She says trying to get him out of his funk.

"I used to be such a jerk. It's no wonder I became this. Now my outside match the inside." He says sulking.

"Cut it out. I still see you in there. I fell for you and even though you bit me..." She says holding up her arm sarcastically, "I still think you're cute?"

"You're funny." He smiles. "You know I'm not the same guy anymore. I've killed."

"We all have, we're at war."

"Yeah, but I'm not sure I can go on forever like this. I'm a monster," He says standing up and walking away, "I'm sorry."

She can do nothing but watch him go. She hangs her head for a moment before pouring herself back into the house.

Inside, Bobby is pulling the syringe out of Jason's arm and for the first time in hours he begins to calm down and becomes somewhat peaceful. The front door swings open with such force that the handle punches through the drywall behind it. It's Sam with a few of the others behind him.

"We've got company!" Sam says stressed.

"How many?" Alexis asks.

"One."

"One?"

"One, talker!" He replies.

Outside in the street stands the sole talker, with his palms out in front of him. He's surrounded by the converts, ready to fight.

"What are you doing here? Alone?" Alexis asks.

A look around brings a smirk to the decayed man's face. "I've been sent to give you a message from our leader." He takes a step forward up onto the curb. "He wants you to know he has your leader."

Alexis reacts without thinking, and before anyone else can make a move, she pulls a large knife from her belt and with her newfound speed, slices across the dead man's chest causing him to fall to his knees bleeding.

"Where is he?" She shouts into his face.

"You must be one of the daughters. The healer perhaps?" He says still smirking as the dark blood drips from his chest.

"What do you want?" Sam interrupts.

The talker has dipped his fingers into his open gash.

"He…wants one…final battle. He…wants…for…all of this to…come to a…end. He'll meet…your army downtown…right before dusk tomorrow." He says looking down and then right back up at Alexis, "Then, you can all die…like your father."

Alexis has heard enough and swings a final swing relieving the talker's shoulders of his head. As it rolls to a stop in the grass, the nearest manhole cover lifts up out of place. From the hole peeks out a dirty soldier covered in grease and dust. It's Airmen Jones who is with the woman that took Addy. They both look humble with their hands in the air.

"We are just here to talk. I think we can help." Jones says humbly. "Tell them." He urges the woman.

As she steps forward wrenching her hands in fear, she opens her mouth, "I, I am the one that took the little girl."

Alexis, still huffing, gets the look of murder once again in her eyes. She lifts her knife just as Sam steps between them.

"She's human. Not one of them. Calm down."

Alexis pulls back, "Where's my sister?!"

The cowering woman responds, "Her beast, the dog. He followed us and she escaped with him."

"My wife did wrong." Jones interrupts, "She just misses our son. She hasn't been herself since he was bitten." He pauses, "She had to stop him when he attacked her in her sleep." Jones says putting his arm around her as they both tear up. "I blame myself, she was leaving me when it happened."

"Which direction did she head?" Alexis bursts out with.
"Towards the strip. She seemed to be heading this way."
The woman answers humbly.

"Well, it's all going to come to an end soon. They want one
last fight and its survivors take all." Sam says.

"I can help" Jones adds, "I mean I know I only survived the
attack on the air force base because I ran and ended up in
the sewer, but everyone else who stood up to them has
died. Even with your thirty or so converts, you're going up
against a lot and I have nothing else to live for."

"This is different." Sam says, "If you want to help, you need
to get the others down there to fight with us, you know we'll
have an even better chance."

"You know it sounds like an ambush to me?" Jones replies.

"Me too." Says Alexis.

"These things have your father. To me, that means if they
want this battle downtown, we have no choice but to give it
to them." Sam declares.

"I'll get them to help." Jones replies, "The old woman listens
to me because I'm military. I'll tell her this is our only hope.
Here's what we do..."

The battle plan is shared, as they all huddle in the street. A
few moments later, Jones and his wife climb back down into
the sewer.

"We'll get the message to them." Airmen Jones says before closing the lid.

Alexis, looking off towards the strip, returns to the house, while Sam and the others prepare.

CHAPTER TWENTY-FOUR

"I'm worried about Addy." Alexis says holding young Riot. "I mean, I know dad can handle himself and honestly I really feel sorry for them. But Addy, she's so little."

"Well, she does have AI with her and that frigging dog wouldn't let anything happen to her and you know that?" Cindy replies.

"I know." Alexis sighs, "I just want them back, even that dumb dog."

Outside in the front yard, Bobby has gathered everyone.

"We all know where this thing ends. Either it's them or us. That's why I'm asking those of you haven't taken advantage of the supply of serum, to do so."

"Why? So we can be out of it and in pain like Jason?" One of the tourists yells out.

"No, it's not like that. Because he was inoculated prior to infection, we had to adjust the levels. He's resting comfortably now." He responds.

"Are you being treated doc?" One of the few females asks.

Without flinching Bobby lifts the now full needle to his neck. He pauses looking out at them and then realizing he doesn't have to be so dramatic, quickly injects himself in the leg.

He lets out a light wince and then says, "Whose next?"

Back inside, Cindy and the babies have moved to the living room where Jason seems to be moving around.

"Babe, can you hear me?" She asks.

Without warning, he cries out a curdling yell that brings him to his feet and then down to his knees. This sends his startled bride wheeling back. His flesh spiders with the familiar veins as his skin tone fades. His arms bulk up and his clothes get tight. He instantly expands in size and as he lifts his head, his eyes open for the first time and the yellow-blood shot mix spreads.

He collapses back into a ball for a moment before reaching out for the edge of the couch, like a crutch to stand.

"Babe?" Cindy asks while Jason's monstrous new body that stands still and silent for what seems like more than a moment.

"It's me." He finally answers causing her to rush into his massive arms.

As they hug she points out the two babies on the couch.

"You did it babe." He says with a creepy new smile.

"There's more." Cindy says. "Addy's missing, they've taken Mike, and those responsible want us to fight one last fight downtown."

"What the hell?" Jason pulls away, "What do you mean they're missing? What fight?"

"We don't have any more time. Everyone is preparing outside."

Frustrated, Jason flings the door open a little harder than he'd expected.

Outside the crew's reaction to seeing the new Jason is shock and awe. The huddling planners break their formation around Sam and welcome him with dropped jaws and stares.

As Sam reaches out to shake Jason's arm, several of the surrounding man holes covers lift up and out of their bases. The appearance of hands precedes the steady flow of militia bodies. Then, the unexpected happens as the civilian soldiers lift a bagged and bound body from one of the holes. It struggles a moment letting everyone know it's not completely dead, whatever it is.

"So they got the big fella?" The old woman asks making her way to the front of them.

"Yeah, I guess. I'm just getting caught up." Jason answers.

"You look different. Does that change anything?" She asks.

"No."

"Good, because I've been coerced to fight alongside you, only I have to insist you treat my people starting with my son."

"Sure, which ones your son?" Bobby asks looking at the hundreds of people still escaping the underground space.

"That one." She answers pointing to the bag.

Bobby and Jason look at each other and nod. Bobby motions Jason closer to him. "There's not enough serum for all these people? At best we can do half."

Jason nods. "Make due."

A scream from the back of the crowd draws attention. It's followed by a few more screams and a parting of the crowd. Al bursts through the crowd huffing and excited to see the family. Alexis hugs him tightly before looking back down his path.

"Where is she? Where is she?" She says.

A moment later she sees her sister cutting through the yards down the street. But, instead of just Addy heading towards them, she's surrounded by the three extremely menacing jungle beasts.

The crowd's reaction is even more drastic now as they pull back in hurry. The mutated tigers approach, sitting down on either side of the street while the lioness prowls the center. Addy pets her head causing her to let out an unexpected purr from deep down in her throat, it rumbles and echoes through the crowd. Addy steps out in front them and extends her arms to her sister who rushes into sweep her up.

"You're alive!" Alexis says with her face buried in Addy's neck. "And you made some very big friends?"

"We saved each other."

"Are they safe?" Alexis asks setting her sister down.

"They listen to me? But, maybe I should have a little talk with them."

Alexis rolls her eyes. Those familiar with Addy, slowly begin to return for hugs.

In the background, Airmen Jones pulls the guys aside, "I got to warn everyone that if the military gets wind of this, they might take advantage with an air strike."

"He's right." Jason agrees, "If they found out everyone will be in one easily attack-able place, they'll send the bombers in to level us."

"What if we..." Jones says pulling them back into a huddle.

Then, as the rest of the crowd prepares for inoculations Bobby begins to wave his arms.

"I'm sorry. I'm sorry. Everybody listen up. We don't have enough for everybody."

The crowd reacts by shouting.

"Yes we do!" Addy yells out from behind them.

Then up, into the crowd, Addy's back pack is passed to the front. Bobby opens it to see the medicine.

"Well, alright then." He says reaching in and pulling out a whole tray of serum.

"What about dad?" Addy asks.

"He's still out there with Ivan. They're going to have to fight their way back to us." Alexis says before going over to Sam and kissing him on the cheek.

"What's that for?" Sam asks.

"Just in case." Alexis says with a smirk.

CHAPTER TWENTY-FIVE

The ground shakes as if an unearthing of hell is being excavated under their feet. A rumbling sound that is unmistakably that of foot soldiers in the thousands, marching towards the apocalypse.

In the downtown street of Fremont, under the canopy that once shined a variety of entertaining light shows, Jason and the small army gather.

They form a line from casino to casino with the dead and converted creatures up front and the rest filing in behind them. Weapons in hand and eyes trained down the block, they are all breathing heavy in anticipation.

The first visible killers are runners. They burst around the corners with wild eyes and open mouths. Their movements so fast it's almost like seeing the opposite play out in slow motion.

They're followed by a massive wave of the slower crawlers.

A block ahead of them steps out the Japanese General looking even more decayed, if that's possible. He lifts his arm to signal the halt behind him.

Standing only about a block apart, the two armies ready themselves for the push. A quiet calm overcomes the streets, as even the breeze has died.

Then, the fight begins with a growl.

Al leads the beasts out in front. The first runner is met with fangs to its throat as Al leaps up and out at the enemy forerunner.

The much stronger converts knock down the enemy dead two and three at a time. The few that break the forward pushing line are met with sharp steel and fierce teeth. Bullets reign out in a thunderous hail from gunmen positioned on overturned kiosks and gaudy awnings.

Jason is smashing skulls with his new found strength and confidence, while Sam fights off two crawlers at once.

Alexis is standing on the corner curb slicing everything in half that approaches her. As she pulls her blade from a split skull, she looks over and sees Sam being snuck up on from behind. She doesn't hesitate diving over a small group that is wrestling in the street. There she lands with her feet firmly planted in the perfect position for a quick hard swing at the ravenous monster, just as it leaps in to attack.

At the same time from behind, a massive undead man lifts its huge arms. Its solid fists are preparing to smash her from behind, while her focus is in front of her. Sam sees this and yells out causing her to half turn, but not in time to defend herself.

As the eminent swing comes down, it's only thwarted by the sudden clasping of the converted lion's jaw on the dead man's thick wrist. It drags the dead man out of position with its momentum and only releases its grip to tear into the big crawlers face.

Both beastly tigers try to help, but bodies from all sides close in on the pile and soon the proud jungle beasts are overwhelmed and quickly dismembered.

Death is everywhere.

Meanwhile, still at the top of the tallest structure in Las Vegas, Michael stands overlooking the destroyed city. He's bloody and bruised and surrounded by Hans' newest breed of talkers.

"I'm conflicted with you. You're group is the only one to make a significant breakthrough with the formula." Hans tells Michael as he begins circling him, "But, then again you have brought great stress to my mission and for this I want you to die, but not until your family and children do. This means I want you to wallow as I take your head."

Michael stands tall, looking out the side of his eye at the scientist's parade. He doesn't yet speak a single word and instead folds his arms in a defiant protest.

"There's nothing you can do to stop me. Your little rebellious run is over. This I promise you."

A crooked smile comes over Michael's face, "We'll see." He responds staring firmly at the ground.

CHAPTER TWENTY-SIX

The splatter of skull fragments and contaminated ooze sprays a nearby lighted frame featuring a free buffet advertisement.

All over the streets the battle continues.

Teeth to face, sword to spleen, and bullet to brain, there seems to be no end to the killing as the mad fever of war has overtaken them all.

The outnumbered crew has done well to thin down the evil army, but it's not enough. Their numbers are too many and it's now forced them into a circle formation as they fight out in all directions. In the distance, the sound of airplane engines boom in the sky.

Alexis and Sam are back to back destroying anything that gets within a few feet of them. Swinging arms and thrusting kicks start to slow as those unconverted begin to tire, but refuse to stop moving.

The masses collapse on them harder and harder, when all of a sudden from around the corner the old army truck comes barreling over a kiosk meant for grilling kabobs. The impact severs a gas line and shoots flames out the sides of the quickly passing over metal machine.

Cindy's, at the wheel, rams through the crowd of pulse-less people. Dr. Bobby is in the passenger seat, buckled in, but hanging out the window. He's swinging a cricket bat at any passing skull he can reach. The babies sit between them, strapped in and bundled up in some sort of gaudy, semi-shiny material that may or may have not been some sort of flamboyant curtain.

As the truck breaks through the bulk of the crowd, Cindy starts to zigzag so that to take out as many of the lifeless threats as possible.

In the center of the converted warriors a manhole lifts out and slides over and Airmen Jones peaks out from inside the hole. Behind him, his wife looks extra worried and quickly disappears back into the darkness.

Jones pulls out a metal device about the same size as a small shoe box. He flips a switch on the electronic device causing it to blink. He then tosses it out into the street, right in the center of the battling crowd.

No one seems to notice it, as the bodies continue falling all around it.

Meanwhile, back on top of the hotel tower Hans' men have begun to grow anxious again. They've begun to try intimidating Michael while waiting for their next orders.

A large, fat dead with a half, chewed-off face has what's left of his nose pressed up against Michael's cheek and he's ranting.

"He thinks he's better than us. He thinks he's right and we're wrong. He thinks he can beat us all."

The words cause the others to become even more agitated, as the group presses in on Michael tighter and tighter. Some even start to take cheap shots, but this does nothing, but work Michael up into his own frenzy and he's now growling and clinching his fists in a tense state.

With both hands pressed against the tilted window that's overlooking the entire valley, Hans has his focus on the downtown areas where the battle is taking place. Then, out from those congested buildings shoots a single flame. This puts a smile on the dead man's rotting face.

"It seems that the time for your friends and family has nearly come and gone."

"What does that mean?" Michael asks with anger in his tone.

"I was to get a signal when we had them surrounded." Hans laughs pointing to the flame.

This sparks something in Michael that he can no longer contain. He lashes out; violently breaking free from the crowd that encircles him.

He puts his fist through what's left of the fat ones skull, dropping his body to its knees. Then, with the blurry speed of the quickest runner, Michael begins to tear through the dead thugs. The once popular mile high tourist destination quickly becomes littered with bodies. The crashing of broken kiosks and shattered restaurant windows fill the air. He splatters a pair against the wall while the two he just finished off bleed out on the ground.

Hans stands back watching the mayhem. Then, as Michael drops the last body to floor, he turns his attention to him.

"You son of a bitch, this whole friggin' thing, you

constructed all of this for your own selfish reason and now it's going to cost you exactly what its cost me." Michael says walking over shattered debris in the direction of the unmoved scientist.

When he's just a few steps away, he's confronted by the last beast he thought would betray him, Ivan, who steps out from the elevator hall and stands between him and Hans.

"What are you doing?" Michael asks confused.

"I can't let you hurt him. I've been made to protect him." Ivan replies.

"You've also sworn to fight with me."

"I know." Ivan says with disdain in his tone, "I'm glad you treated me with the serum. It's given me a clean enough head to remember my objectives."

"He uses people. First the scientists to create this hell and now he's using you to expand it!" Michael says pointing to Hans.

"I'll never be normal again. Neither will you. You fight for what you used to be. Not what you are." Ivan barks back.

"I fight for my family." Michael says getting into his face.

Off in the distance the formation of the final fighter jets break the horizon. The glare off one of the wings draws Michael's eye over Ivan's shoulder.

Ivan turns his head to see the same thing.

"Now, your family will die." Ivan says with his head still turned.

Michael takes a crushing swing knocking Ivan back on his ass. Without hesitation Michael pounces on him with fire in his eyes. He throws blow after violent blow until the veiny gray colored flesh that was Ivan's face, is pummeled back into almost a rosy, lifelike shade. Pushing off the motionless Ivan, Michael stands and grabs his limp body by his upper jaw and begins to drag him. He moves straight for the now backing up Hans. A final, violent yank pulls the whole top of Ivan's head off from the jaw up.

"This..." Michael says shaking the half skull, "This is the army you brought to terrorize us. Is this the best you have? I promise you, I am going to hunt down every last one of them into extinction."

"But not before it costs you your entire family." Hans says with a smile.

Michael's eyes narrow as he tosses the skull at Hans' before grabbing him by the waist line and neck and lifting him up into the air. A kick of the glass door that separates them from the outer deck allows Michael to carry out his nemesis into the open air.

As he prepares to toss the psycho to his eminent true death, the sneaky bastard pulls a knife from his belt and plunges it into Michael's neck causing him to drop the crazed mad man short of the ledge.

"So much talk..." Hans starts to say, but only gets out the first part of his sentence before Michael rises up to grab him again by the throat.

"Then shut up!" Michael says tossing Hans off the insanely high roof.

The momentum from tossing Hans over the ledge leaves him leaning over in the perfect position to watch as the evil man tumbles back, swimming in the air on his way to his imminent death.

Blood drips from the knife still stuck in Michael's shoulder. He removes it and drops it to the ground.

CHAPTER TWENTY-SEVEN

Thundering engines grow louder as the fighter planes drop altitude and hone in on the target area.

On the ground, the Japanese General stands defiantly in the center of the street glaring up.

Michael, being on the observation deck, is high enough to witness the hell.

Just then, the planes clamps release multiple bombs that hobble towards earth. The blast lights up the cities landscape, setting everything in the vicinity of downtown, on fire.

Michael falls to his knees as the wall of flames rise into the skyline. The blinding blaze reflects in his widened eyes as he crumbles in a whimper, his dry sockets unable to form tears. He collapses to his knees.

The sun begins to quickly go down. The smoldering buildings seep smoke and the glow of orange and red embers are causing deep shadows to form everywhere.

Michael stumbles to his feet grasping the rail. He pauses a moment and then turns to head towards the elevator almost drunk with depression.

As the elevator doors close around him, the pain begins to manifest physically. He pounds the steel walls with his fists as the drool streams from his lips like he's gone rabid. His heavy breathing and abrupt grunt echo around the metal walls in stereo.

When the doors split open around him, he steps out into the battle worn casino. The loud crunch of fallen debris under his boot drawls the attention of a lone deranged crawler.

The empty pit in Michael's chest rushes to his brain as he attacks for the first time teeth first. Not out of an urge, but out of pure anger and revenge driven hatred.

Bite after bite, Michael feasts on the undead flesh.

TO WHOM IT MAY CONCERN:

The situation in Las Vegas is grave.

I've thrown the mastermind of this mess off the top of the tallest building in the city, but I couldn't find his body. I've run into several of the undead in my search through the rubble. Most of them alone and wondering. My urge to hurt the thing that infects them has grown into something dangerously un-human.

The taste of rotting flesh has become something I crave the more I think about my little girls. It's like biting into a skull or ripping into one of their chest cavities brings on a euphoric type of satisfaction or revenge and even though it only last seconds, it's the only thing I can feel anymore.

I searched for the bodies of my family and friends, but they must have been completely cremated in the blast. Even the metal of the surrounding cars and manhole covers have been melted from the immense heat.

It's this finality that has me heading down my current path. I vowed to hunt down and kill every one of these frigging things. Only now, it's my new hunger for their flesh that will be their demise. I will do unto them, as they've done to me...

- Michael, cannibal.

BREAKING NEWS TELEVISION BROADCAST

"We have breaking news to report to you tonight. It seems the sole flight to escape the havoc taking place in the once vibrant tourist capital of Las Vegas, Nevada has made an emergency landing in Chicago, Illinois. We want to take you live to the scene of this nearly tragic event."

A row of press cameras have set up alongside the small road that runs parallel to the runway. Only a five foot chain link fence and a small patch of grass separate the reporters from the wounded plane.

As it lies there lifeless on its belly and smoking from its engines, the reporters are all lined up and yammering into their respective cameras.

"Tom, we've gathered just outside the runway of this incredible sight. Earlier tonight, flight 311 out of Las Vegas made an emergency landing, sliding to a halt where it lies."

The focus now shifts to the plane itself.

"We're showing you live footage of the fire and rescue teams breaching the hull for the first time. Hopefully, the passengers inside will be safe and accounted for. We don't have any word yet, as communication with the plane has been nonexistent since its take off." The reporter pauses as the torch being used to cut open the hatch goes dark, "Oh, it looks like there is some activity, let's watch."

The door is popped open and the rescuers all pull back covering their noses from what appears to be a horrible smell.

"Can we zoom in?" The reporter asks his cameraman.

Then, as the workers poke their heads into the plane, the sudden rush of disgusting dead knocks them back and off the stairway. As the monsters hit the ground they violently begin latching onto everyone in their path.

The press is frozen with fear, as the runners break off, leaving the crawlers behind to pick the bones. The monsters head straight for the lit up fence and shocked reporters.

Then, just as they breach the fence, the runners pounce the cameramen causing the news reports to, one by one across America, to go black.

LAS VEGAS, NEVADA
DEVASTATED DOWNTOWN AREA

Meanwhile, back on the streets of downtown Las Vegas, the destruction and debris blow slightly in the breeze. In the center of the street, the melted edges of the manhole cover are cooled and firm.

Smoke begins to creep out the holes in the lid as a familiar hissing sound comes from under the ground.

Then, there is silence.

In a boom, the lid is blown up into the air landing several feet away, in a spin.

PART THREE

DEAD END

TO WHOM IT MAY...forget it,

In my current state, I don't have enough emotions left in my body to share anything more than a warning.

I am filled with hatred and overflowing with anger. I am void of compassion. I now only have revenge on my heart and a taste for their blood on my lips.

Be warned, if any undead man crosses my path, I will devour him with a fury that only Satan himself would find comfortable witnessing.

You've taken my family, ravaged my body, and now you'll take what I have for you in return.

Enough talk...I suggest anything void of a heartbeat should run and hide!

Michael, hunter

CHAPTER TWENTY-EIGHT

The sun comes up over the Las Vegas valley and the devastation that has ravished through the city is evident on each and every street and on every corner. Neighborhood homes and business storefronts alike look as if they've partied hard and violently thrown up their content into the streets.

The roads are quiet and irregular gusts of wind move debris and loose political posters around on the surface of this once packed tourist haven. There seems to be no witnesses left of the events.

An out of place, yet familiar, sound hisses in the distance.

Without warning, a spurt of smoke begins to force its way out through the small cracks on several of the melted manhole implanted in the downtown street. As the smokes dies down there is a moment of silence that is then followed up by sudden and forceful explosions. One by one the warped lids fly up and out of their once solid resting places and into the air ten feet only to land with a thud and slowly spin to a stop.

Meanwhile, the phenomenon of empty streets continues for miles and miles outside the valley.

Back in Kingman, Arizona the cold, lifeless train sits as a reminder of the hell it unleashed on the quiet townspeople. In the background, the ravaged community looks like a ghost town. A few stray cats are roaming around, some are scavenging for food. A loud mechanical sound comes from the front of the train. It seems to have been on a timer that has brought it back to life.

A second, different grinding sound comes from the first passenger car, then the second. This continues down the line like that of dominoes falling for what seems like miles.

Then, each car automatically re-engages and on its own the train begins to slowly move.

STATELINE NEVADA/UTAH BORDER

A stretch of interstate that at one point the only way out of the contaminated area has since been evacuated by its once loyal locals and has now become the final resting place for those who thought they could tough it out.

Unfortunately, it was also one of the first places that stragglers arrived looking for a human meal.

Movement under some of the trash stirs up various pieces of litter on the street. Posters for presidential candidate Joseph Smith hang half torn off a temporary billboard mounted in front of the town's now empty gun store.

The wheel of an overturned motorcycle with California license plates comes to a stop in the middle of the empty street, its rider huffs a low growl and crawls around the concrete confused. His skin has become gray and riddled with those familiar heavy veins. He's showing all the obvious signs that point to the fact that he must have been attacked while riding through the epicenter. He must have begun transforming somewhere between there and here and now it's just too late.

The biker's radio is playing static filled classic rock in the background.

As the shops front door slams open from the force of the undead body being flung out of it, Michael steps out and over the corpse crushing a random campaign pin under his boot. The biker looks up at the commotion as a long stream of saliva drips from the corner of his infected mouth. Michael sees the overturned bike and fresh dead and doesn't hesitate to attack and destroy the virgin crawler.

As he bites one last chunk out of the dead man's face, his hand grips the ground under the pool of contaminated blood flowing out the lifeless body. He lifts himself to his feet and looks over and sees the man's bike and stands it up. He wipes the blood from his mouth with his sleeve and pushes a button on the radio and a much clearer station tunes in. It's an ad for Smith's candidacy.

"I have a plan to make America safe again. I would put measures in place that would protect the public and alleviate these problems we face."

His words are followed with breaking news from Chicago about the emergency plane landing and subsequent spread of terror that took place there as well as the apparent report of incidents along the planes path.

"We've been getting reports from small towns across the country, about more and more infections taking place. We want to ensure you that we're going to continue bringing you the latest developments, as soon as they're reported."

Michael climbs on the bike and flips a button to start the motorcycle. As he pulls away from the small town, it can't help but reminds him of his town.

When he reaches the end of the border town, he makes a half-hearted attempt to look back on what he's leaving behind in his path. The look on his scarred face is somewhere between sadness and screaming out.

He doesn't make a sound.

He simply grinds his teeth as he shifts gears and rides off into the horizon, soaked in the blood of the dead he's killed.

CHAPTER TWENTY-NINE

FLAGSTAFF, ARIZONA

A cute girl dressed in short cut off jean shorts walks up to a greasy mechanic who is working on what is obviously her pink and black eco-friendly mini car.

"So, how much longer?" She asks never looking away from the smart-phone screen she's tapping away at.

"Well, you're in luck. The problem was electrical and I was able to pull a few favors and found you the only replacement part for a hundred miles. Only problem is that they don't give us much room to work on these little things, so it's been sort of a bitch repairing it." He says pulling his hand out to show her his bloody knuckles.

"Oh, no." she replies at the sight.

"No worries princess, I'll have you out of here and back on spring break in no time."

A block away, and in clear view of the station, the ghost train rumbles to a stop.

A lead-lined box, inside the first car, is triggered to open exposing an electromagnetic device that has three lights set up in a stop light pattern.

The first green light is lit up. After a minute goes by the yellow light flips on.

Back at the auto shop, the mechanic is sitting in the driver's seat of the little car. After a moment of silent prayer, the mechanic turns the key to start the engine. He instantly rejoices at the cars cooperation by smacking the steering wheel grinning ear-to-ear.

Suddenly, the electric instruments in his shop start acting funny as all the lights begin to flicker as a wave of energy tears through the town forcing everything electronic in its path to fry out. The town goes dark. The girl smacks her phone trying to revive it, as the mechanic throws a fit.

Once again, the train engages and moves on methodically heading east.

LAS VEGAS, NEVADA

Back in burnt out remains of Las Vegas, the smoke has cleared from what is left of the downtown area. The blown out hole cover lies off in the distance as survivors are now emerging from the sub-terrain. By now, each of the family members has made their way out, into the light. It's only now, in this moment, that they can finally see the aftermath of the napalm blasts and how it's melted most of the area.

"Do you think he's still alive?" Addy asks.

"If anyone of us was ever going to survive up here, it would be your dad." Cindy adds trying to reassure her niece.

"We need to form a few small search crews to spread out and look for him and whoever or whatever else is left." The monstrous looking Jason says to Cindy who is holding one of her young children.

She nods in agreement.

Alexis, overhearing this, smacks Sam on the back as she passes him heading in the direction of the strip.

"Come on, dead man." She adds, "We'll go this way."

But, before they can get too far, swarms of heavily armed soldiers begin to drop from the dozen or so helicopters that have appeared and are now hovering overhead.

"What do these guys want?" Alexis asks out loud, "Where were you yesterday, assholes?"

"We're here for you own safety." one of them barks out with an assault rifle pointing in their direction.

"Seriously?" Sam says with a rebellious tone. Something Alexis has grown to like about him.

Now, before he elevates the situation, Jason puts himself between the soldiers and the survivors.

"Fine," He adds speaking for everyone as they surrender, "We're on the same team."

UNKNOWN, USA

Meanwhile, out on the road, Michael has made good time and is approaching a new town. He looks down at the gauges on his motorcycle and notices that he's almost out of gas. He pulls into the next station he comes to.

As he comes to a stop, he discovers that even this far from Vegas, the town seems to be abandoned.

Inside the small gas station, Michael finds the place looks like it has been turned upside down. As he turns the corner, to look for the pump switch, he finds an entire family looks to have been devoured by what can only be a group of dead. A look of anger comes over Mike's face, as he sees what he assumes is the remains of a child and young girl in the pile of bodies.

Michael loses control at the sight and tears out through the door and into the street to find who is responsible. As he stands grimacing, looking for a clue of which direction to go, he catches a whiff of who he's looking for, and they're not too far away.

He follows the scent around the back of a small set of buildings where he finds three crawlers feasting on what looks like a heavy-set grandmother.

As Michael prepares to attack, a whizzing sound comes from the sky. Unconcerned, Michael shrugs it off when he sees that it is just some sort of remote spy drone flying overhead.

UNDISCLOSED BASE, USA

Inside an undisclosed secret base, the family is being shown the footage from the drone. At first, they all hug one another and seem relieved to see Michael alive. Then, as he proceeds to attack the three dead in a way they've never witnesses, Addy cover's her eyes and buries her face in Alexis' shoulder.

After a minute she peeks out and sees the pain on her father's face, and knows there is something more going on.

"He thinks we're dead. He's not himself." She says.

"I believe that might just be the case, young lady." Says a mysterious man in a business suit who is hanging out behind them, "You see, not only is he heading east, so is an unmanned train that is equipped with EMP's that are knocking out power all across the country. What's worse, at some point the darn thing separated into smaller sets of self-propelled cars and has spread out into so many directions that stopping them, aside from being a logistical nightmare, could actually cause more damage than solution? Especially, because we can't move forward without causing even more civilian casualties."

Alexis begins to pace back and forth, "We have to go get him!" She approaches the man, "We could get him to stop. He sees us alive and he'll quit and come with us."

With a snicker, the man doesn't reply.

"But, we don't want him to stop." A familiar voice says out of the shadows.

Unfortunately, no one can see who it is, but the military man excuses himself to meet with the mysterious man in the darkness.

CHAPTER THIRTY

The dark, inner workings of the government compound seem cold and inhumane, the type of place where devious activities are planned and deceitful men come to carry them out.

The family, minus Al and Lea the lioness, are worn out and being held in a windowless room. There is nothing in the room but a stainless steel conference table, a dozen matching chairs, a pitcher of water, and a stack of paper cups.

Cindy catches a glimpse of Jason's profile and notices he isn't looking as dead as he once did.

"Either I'm going crazy or the light in here was designed to be flattering. You're looking better." Cindy can't help but mention.

"I'm feeling more like myself for the first time since I changed." He answers.

In a makeshift lab of sorts, set up away from the family, the mystery military man walks in to find the rest of the dead converts chained and Al and Lea are in cages.

As the mystery man stares into the cages he asks, "How come the uncle and the boyfriend aren't in here?"

Someone unidentified answers back in a heavy German accent, "Because, they're part of the family and if we separated them, their focus would be shifted."

"The government controls the military for the most part, but with his family we can control this one." Smith speaks out from the other side of the room, while pointing to a still shot of Michael on a monitor, "Spin him as a hero working for us when the president's military refuses to act on the behalf of the real American's, and we come off golden."

"That's good. Good enough to turn this whole thing back around." Hans says finally revealing he's alive.

"That's why I'm the face of this whole..." Smith says pausing to find the right word, "...thing?"

Meanwhile, back out in the world, Michael has moved on another town, closer to his Chicago destination.

"I am crazy." Michael tells himself as he stares into the reflection he sees in an old truck window, "I'm just another goddamn monster."

A scream from down the street interrupts his thoughts and without thinking he rushes in its direction. It's another pocket of dead and this time the killers are chasing some teens across a field.

In the field, Mike finds what looks like flattened bodies that have obviously fallen from the sky. It looks as if they have landed all around a shallow pond that might have been occupied when they impacted.

"They threw infected bodies from the plane." Michael mumbles looking up at the sky.

Another scream refocuses his attention back on the hunt.

Mike quickly catches the two slower crawlers who look to have been only teenagers themselves. He swiftly decapitates them both and continues on.

Once he reaches the runner, it's too late for an unfortunate fat kid it was pursuing as he's now in the process of being devoured. Michael interrupts the attack by biting into the back of the speedster's neck and tearing away a huge mouthful of flesh. He stomps out the beast while its victim transforms. He then, without missing a beat and getting emotional again, turns and gorges himself on the newly created runner before it can even take its first step.

Michael's anger forces him to continue eating flesh until he's exhausted and passes out in a flesh induced stupor.

For the first time since his conversion, he falls into a dream state.

At first he sees nothing but a white, heaven-like canvass. This entire world is blank and as he turns around he sees the vastness continues on into nothingness until in the distance he can make something out. Then as he gets closer to whatever it is, he can see that it's his father's old oak kitchen table and the same table that is sitting in his home right now. It is messy and looks like it is probably just the way they left it before this whole nightmare began.

He pulls out the old chair he used to sit in and settles into his old spot. He slowly lays his spread palms on its surface and bends down to press his face into the mess.

He breathes in deeply and doesn't move.

CHAPTER THIRTY-ONE

Mike awakes groggy and to the sight of the mysterious military man leaning against the aged red brick that lines the alley. There is an uncomfortable silence that feels almost like that moment in the wild before two rivals pounce on one another for dominance.

The man's arms unfold as he raises a single finger.

"You are amazing. You know, you have become something that no one ever saw coming. You have become this all-American hero, who's undergone this transformation that now has the world fixated. Not just because they enjoy the thrill of watching you man-handle their nightmares, but because they see you as their only true protector."

Michael makes his way up onto his knees. His head is down as he positions himself to stand.

"We want to harness this power you have, and focus it on getting you to back Mr. Smith for president." There is another pause, "I know this is a difficult request, but I think we might just have something you want in exchange."

For the first time, in what feels like forever, Michael senses something in the man's demeanor that indicates he's done his homework on Michael.

"Yeah, what?" Michael growls.

"You help us, and we'll give you your kids back."

"My kids are dead!" Michael rages to his feet and immediately plunging towards the man, who doesn't flinch, and instead a single shot reigns out from the roof above. It grazes Mike's shoulder as a warning and ricochets off the ground between the two.

"You will be surprised at just how strong concrete and manhole covers really are." The man adds.

Grabbing his shoulder to feel for blood, Mike agrees, "What do I have to do?"

"Just keep doing what you're doing." The man responds.

Mike's face turns to stone, as he turns to walk away. The man, seeing that Mike is receptive, makes a call on his cell, "It's a go."

Back at the base, and on the other end of the phone call, a soldier shakes his head and makes a sign to a small group of men encompassing the family.

One soldier speaks up, "Gather your belongings; It looks like you won't be staying with us any longer. It's now at this point the US government would like to offer you all of our apologies for the inconvenience."

"What about the rest our people?" Jason asks.

"They've been moved. Once the infection is figured out and they have been treated, they'll be released."

"I want my animal friends back!" Addy demands.

After a brief pause, and an emotionless stare, the soldier

whispers to the guard standing next to him. The guard disappears momentarily and returns a few minutes later. He whispers back into soldiers ear an obvious response to the request.

"The ones that remain will be in the vehicle we're sending you all home in."

"Is one of them Al?" Addy pleas, "Tell, me! Is my dog okay? Is he one of them?"

At this point, both Jason and Sam exchange looks of hesitation, but remain silent.

CHAPTER THIRTY-TWO

Small towns across America have been left desolate and dark after the ghost trains rolled through unleashing blast after blast. Most small communities have been left to fend for themselves, in the dark. The truly unlucky have been invaded and ravished by newly created dead and their warm welcome to this new world is an arm out, teeth first type of approach.

Of those towns lucky enough to only lose their power, they've gotten wind of the unlucky ones through privately-funded, emergency supply drops that include a littering of propaganda-like fliers. This latest series show Michael killing a runner with the caption, "Because the military refuses to act, we will" and a very obvious 'paid for' panel asking for the support of Mr. Smith's presidential candidacy.

An SUV filled with the newly released family, creeps through the streets looking for clues of Michael's whereabouts.

"So, we know where he's going, just not where he's at now." Jason mentions breaking the silence.

"Well, if he's going to Chicago that's where we need to be." Alexis adds.

As they turn off the town's main street towards the freeway, they see flattened bodies scattered throughout the landscape.

On the side of the road, they find infected body after body mangled and dead, only these are obviously ones Mike killed passing through.

"He's been this way, look." Jason says pointing at the bodies.

Cindy is feeding Rowan, while Riot seems just like a normal baby, playing with the strap on his father's gun. As she looks over she sees Jason's silhouette, she does another double take. He almost appears completely human to her? She looks back at Sam and sees that, he too seems to be getting better.

Lexi notices the look on her aunt's face and acknowledges Cindy's discovery by lifting a single eyebrow while she continues sharpening a knife.

In the back of the truck, Addy and Al are leaning on each other. Al is enjoying the wind in his face, while "Bennie" the tiger, as he's been nicknamed, is resting at her feet.

Addy smiles at the sight of Al's lips flapping in the wind.

Out of nowhere, a unexpected explosion in the road causes the truck to swerve off to the side. A second explosion on the other side of the road sends the truck back the other way with a jerk that's so hard, no one is left unscathed.

As they come to a screeching stop, they are once again surrounded by armed men. Only this time it's not the same men, these guys are private security for hire and they're being led by the mysterious military man.

As the men approach, the truck doors slowly open and

one-by-one everyone files out. Alexis looks back into the truck and sees Addy has been knocked unconscious from the commotion. At the same time, both Al and Bennie seem to acknowledge this too an both animals jump down out from the back of truck and prepare to attack.

"Hey, call your pets or we'll shoot." says one of the armed men.

"They aren't going to listen to us. They're my sister's pets and they're very protective of her." Alexis adds.

As the two beasts encroach on the men, the impending attack has the men a little jumpy. Bennie makes the first move, he's shot repeatedly in midair, but he keeps coming and kills off his assailant with a single bite.

"No!" Lexi yells, as Sam holds her back.

Al is right behind him, but stops his attack and backs up defensively between the men and Addy, when he sees them moving in.

"I thought you let us go?" Lexi asks.

"I have other plans for you." says the Military Man stepping out from behind the crowd.

"You see, you are all pawns in a little game we're playing." says Presidential hopeful Mr. Smith who is revealed to be standing next to the Military Man.

Al's growl remains steady, as the men continue to hold the group hostage.

"Everyone in the transports," orders one of the rent-a-soldiers, "No pets."

CHAPTER THIRTY-THREE

"I'm almost there. I can smell the death; it's like a primal aphrodisiac of sorts to me now." Michael thinks to himself as he pulls to a stop on the outskirts of a small town trailer park.

When Mike attempts to continue on, the engine on his stolen bike gives out. As he tries to start it again, he realizes it is out of gas. Stepping off and letting the bike drop where it stands, he makes his way into the dilapidated trailer park.

Right away he notices this is no regular white trash community. There are signs that appear to have been written in blood and weird voodoo like relics tied to the doorways and trees.

As trippy as this initial scene plays out, the sight of freak show memorabilia and circus equipment makes the setting more apparent.

"Gypsy circus?" He mumbles to himself.

As the revelation of his environment begins to sink in, he realizes he's yet to see anyone dead or alive. A noise from behind has him turning to investigate. Just as he does, an old woman who has long been turned dead leaps out at him. She seems to be chanting something under her breath, as if she's retained the abilities of one of the talkers.

As he tries to pry her monkey like grip from around his neck, he's pounced on by at least a dozen other oddities.

In a rage of adrenaline, Michael knocks everyone back and tears into the old woman teeth first, severing her head from her shoulders. Just as her head hits the ground a tattooed man picks up the same chant. Mike reaches through the dead man's chest and pulls out a hand full of guts. He takes a bite of the entrails while staring into the man's yellowed eyes.

A woman with a face full of hair bites down on Michael's shoulder and two of the tiniest dead twins attempt to bite into his legs. In a fit, he crushes the man's skull, flips the woman over his shoulder and onto her back. He kicks the two tiny people so hard that, one of them pops as it impacts a nearby tree.

Again, in a horrific manner, Mike gorges himself on flesh and again as he reaches a state of fullness he realizes he might have a chance of revisiting his dream state. So, he continues to feast until he collapsing into his alternate universe.

His once blank world has now manifested itself in more detail. He pauses to take in a deep breath, realizing it seems as if it's been an eternity since he took in the sight of those enormous trees outside his house.

"Is that really how blue the trim on the house is?" He asks himself.

As he turns around to take in the scenery, additional details begin to unfolding right before his eyes. Returning to face the house, he catches his reflection in the front window. He's himself, not a monster. His clear skin and bright blue eyes stand out and cause him to almost gasp.

"The girls?" He asks, realizing the possibility that they might be here. He runs through the yard and into the house, "Girls!"

There is no reply.

As a matter of fact, there is no sound in the home at all. He quickly bursts out the back door and into the surrounding streets. There are no people, no animals, not even a bug!

As he runs through this other world, he realizes all the lifeless details. Then, without knowing its origin, he can hear the sound of the song, 'Nowhere to Run, Nowhere to Hide' begin to play in the background.

Suddenly, he awakes to the screeching sound of an old radio hanging off the porch of one of the trailers.

It proceeds to play an announcement, "To any survivors," its Smith's voice, "I have taken measures to assist our small town people in this time of 'infected' crisis. Since no cure has been found and these things, dubbed "runners, crawlers, and talkers" by the online community, threaten us all, I have teamed with the monster killer known simply as Michael. Now is the time to fight fire with fire. It is not time to quarantine and wait like the current president is attempting to do. It's that approach that is costing more uninfected lives by the day, and the sealing off of Chicago is just one more sign that our current leader doesn't know what he's doing. Look for more aerial food supply drops coming, at my own personal expense, and additional detailed materials regarding our mission to keep you all safe. I've made this my personal duty because no one else has. I am Candidate Smith, and I approve this message."

As the signal returns to static, then silence, Michael finally sits up to be face-to-face with a large, gray wolf who has been preserved through taxidermy. It instantly reminds him of Al, and this causes him to think about Addy and Lex.

"Nothing will stop this pain; I'll never get them back." He mumbles to himself.

The horrific and surreal events and these vivid dreams play through his mind in fast forward. It's obvious that it is becoming impossible to tell the difference between what's fake and what's real. His dark green and gray, vein filled skin is bulging and trembling. It is in these slight moments of silence that he can't help but to be filled with rage.

A noise comes from off in the distance and he rises to his feet to attack whatever it is. But, just as he turns the corner he sees what looks like Addy turning the next corner.

He yells, but all he seems to be able to let out is an odd growl. He rushes to catch up, but it's too late, when he rounds the next corner, whoever he saw is gone.

CHAPTER THIRTY-FOUR

Confused, Michael stands panting and out of breath from the stress. He's leaning up against the brick wall in the alley and his mind is racing and nothing is making sense. Again, he hears a noise. Only this time it's a louder scuffling like that of a dozen or so feet. He turns and sees a small group of dead walk by. They seem to be what is left of the local police department and from the rate they're moving, they're crawlers.

Michael takes his first step and accidentally kicks an empty beer can, alarming the crawler crew. This causes them to turn and growl. Michael takes their acknowledgment as aggression and is sent into a frenzy.

He rushes them.

As the fighting begins, Michael is immediately double teamed by two of the infected beasts who seem to have retained some of their training. As one attempts to choke him, the other wrestles his waist. Flipping the first crawler over his shoulder and pinning it to the ground by its neck under his boot, he sees something out of the corner of his eye.

From the same alley he just investigated, he sees Alexis standing at the opening of it with no emotion on her face. She stands there for a moment as if she's watching him, then slowly turns and disappears.

Puzzled, Michael tears the crawler from his waist and stomps through the skull of the other while pushing through the rest in an attempt to rush over towards her.

Again, he finds nothing.

He frantically searches more thoroughly, ripping open doors on random trailers and knocking over anything she could be behind. But, still he finds nothing. Then, he hears his sister calling him and his newborn niece and nephew crying in the distance. Huffing at the air, he tries to pursue the sound, but he is left spinning.

He stops his search and instead falls to his knees confused and out of his mind.

When the dead, that were left alive, catch up mindlessly, Michael is in no mood. He lunges at the hoard, biting his way through them in the most gruesome of ways.

Splatters of blood and an abundance of entrails are strewn about mercilessly.

CHAPTER THIRTY-FIVE

Michael is on his knees and in obvious internal anguish as he claws at his own head trying to release the pain.

Off in the distance sits two military jeeps filled with both his family and the team of military men. They've been watching the events.

"You're torturing him." Addy says.

"No, we're motivating him." A soldier replies.

Addy can't stand to look anymore and buries her head as the driver starts the engine and pulls away and down the road.

"What do you think they're going to do with us?" Cindy asks Jason in a whisper.

"I'm not sure. They've got something big planned." He replies.

Meanwhile, Alexis is trying to comfort her sister and looks over to Sam. He smiles, but she sees a commotion in the bushes behind him in the passing scenery. She's keeps focused on the brush and sees it again.

She signals Sam with her eyes to look behind him. Confused at first he turns to look out the window. Then, with one more appearance they realize just what it is.

It's Al.

Alexis taps Addy on the top of her head to get her attention. She silently directs her to look out the window, just as Al pops up from the row of bushes lining the roadside.

"He's following us." Addy whispers.

Alexis smiles and the two hug.

Without warning, and from the other side of the road, Bennie the tiger jumps out in front of the caravan. Startled, the first driver swerves causing the second driver to follow.

As they hit the dip in the side of the road, both vehicles go airborne and the first vehicle begins to flip uncontrollably as the second jeep, carrying the family, crashes to its side and slides to a stop near some trees.

As the men fall out and crawl from the damaged wrecks, both Al and Bennie go on the attack. Bite, after fierce bite, leave man after man grasping at their gaping wounds.

All the upheaval allows the girls enough time to escape into the woods. Then, just as the second driver takes aim to fire into the area of the fleeing family, Bennie lunges at the man taking the shot through his open mouth and out the back of his head. Stunned the mercenary unloads his clip into Bennie, killing him instantly. Thinking he's survived, the man takes his last breath as Al, in a full sprint, leaps and tears his head from his shoulders while in pursuit to join Addy.

As they make their way through the woods, both Addy and Al stop as the sound of pursuing gunfire reaches them. Al whimpers and Addy holds her mouth.

"Addison!" Lexi yells noticing she's stopped running, "What are you doing?"

"They got Bennie. I know it, they got him."

"Sweetie, we can't stop." Alexis pleas, "We got to keep moving."

It's at this time, for the first time, that Addy looks at Al. His eyes are brown again and even though he's still much larger than he was before he changed, he's never looked so normal since being infected.

From an unknown direction, a shot reigns out intended for the girls. It rips through Al's shoulder and he falls limp.

These aren't normal bullets. These are something else. Something designed for maximum damage.

The world goes into a sort of twisted slow motion, as bullet after bullet tears up the ground and trees around them. Then, as a few strays whiz by Addy's head, Alexis grabs her by the arm just in time to drag her out of the way.

Still focused on Al as she's being hauled away, she sees another bullet tear through Al's side.

"No!" She cries out before beginning to rationalize, "He'll heal! I know it, he'll heal! Wait!"

Dodging and darting through the trees, Cindy looks over and notices Jason is now looking even more human than before as his skin now has more of a fleshy tone to it.

Sam scoops up Addy so that they can move faster. She's in tears, so he holds her tight in attempts to comfort her.

They run until the sun starts to go down.

"Look." Alexis says pointing at a downed road sign that reads:

JOLIET, 1 MILE
CHICAGO, 46 MILE

"We can make that in an hour, if we can get a hold of a vehicle." Sam says.

"Or two days on foot." Jason adds.

"That means he could get there a full day before us?" Cindy asks.

"If he's not already there, it might be more than that." Jason responds.

Unknown to them, Mike has collapsed face down in the dirt. His eyes have rolled back in his head as his latest meal begins to take its effect on his conscious state.

He opens his eyes and finds himself lying in the green grass in his front yard. He can see that there are ants crawling in and out of a small hole near the tree, but the streets are still silent.

In the tree above him he sees what looks like a shadowy figure. As he stands up he notices several figures have now formed in various positions throughout its large branches.

As the first figure starts to manifest into a solid object, it becomes clear that he's only seen this person once before. It's the crazed old woman who led the chanting before he fell out.

She begins to speak like a whisper that is ringing loud in Michael's ears, "You know not the extent of this thing. What was once metaphysical has become flesh and now the flesh feeds. The world is a cycle and this thing cannot remain solely in the blood of the ones that walk. It will breed an evil you have yet to meet. You are just one man and even if you cure the flesh, the door between the two worlds has been opened. It will take one that is pure to close that door and of the two heads that exist, it will take several seasons of darkness before they realize their destiny. So man must adapt into a primitive being if he is to see the end of it all."

Michael is taken back and confused at the cryptic message.

"What does that mean" He asks.

She simply holds what appears to be her finger over her mouth as if to shush him. She then cups her hands and blows what feels like a powerful gust of wind that sends Mike reeling back on his heels.

As he hits the ground, he awakes to the sun cracking the horizon. He stumbles to his feet and sees the carnage he's caused all around him.

Coldly, he steps over the bodies and pulls a gas can off the porch of one of the trailers and shakes it. It's nearly full. He looks over and sees the wicked woman from his dream torn apart and contorted. Her sunken eye sockets seem to be staring right into him. He looks past her.

He returns to the motorcycle that is still lying where he left it. He sets down the can and lifts the bike back upright and kicks down the stand. He twists off the gas lid on the bikes tank and proceeds to empty as much of the gas as it will hold.

He takes the remaining fuel and walks back into the park pouring over the bodies and various other items. He grabs a pack of camping matches that are sitting on an old barbeque and sparks one. As he walks away he drops the match into the box, igniting the entire box into a ball of fire. He tosses the box into the pile of bodies, instantly igniting and spreading through the trailer community.

He mounts the bike and flips the ignition. It doesn't start. He tries again, and it starts up strong. He pulls away towards Chicago.

This time he never looks back.

CHAPTER THIRTY-SIX

CHICAGO, ILLINOIS

The streets of Chicago, and its surrounding boroughs, have been overrun with dead. Runners and crawlers can be found on just about every street. There is no telling just how many talkers are in command now and you'd be hard pressed to find someone who is not infected.

Mike arrives in the outskirts of Chicago, where he finds the slim number of stumbling converts disappointing. He drives through the dozen or so single straggler's as if they were beneath him at this point. He's look for the hordes.

As he pulls up and onto an over pass, he stops and look out towards the downtown area. The look on his face transforms from ambivalence to rage as he's found what he's looking for.

It doesn't take long for him to make his way into meat of the mass of killers. As always, their first impression of Michael is that he's one of them. But, as the smell of his chemically-retained, human-side begins to overcome that initial sense, they become aggressive.

Up until now, Mike has either only encountered a limited numbers of infected souls or has had others with him to endure the fight. Michael's mind is gone and just as his essence triggers his others senses, their essence intoxicates him. Now in a drunken rage, his blood-fed spree has fed this altered state and given him a strength that makes him an uncontrollable threat to their existence.

He makes his way through the crowd, crushing skulls in single swings and tearing flesh from any body part that gets within a foot from his grasp. His style has become more primal as he uses anything around him to kill. He shoves a pipe through ones chest and a hand full of re-bar through several others skulls. His stamina is now fueled with blood and adrenaline as his thirst for revenge is finally being fulfilled.

In only a short time, hundreds are killed and his blood-drunken rage has made him almost unrecognizable. The more he bites through and destroys, the less human he seems as he grunts and slobbers his way through the blood soaked streets.

In the distance, a helicopter is hovering over the city filming the bloodshed. The feed is being broadcast to the world.

NETWORK STUDIO
SOMEWHERE, USA

"With an emergency state being declared across the county and the current president refusing to use military force, it seems the U.S. has a new protector. Presidential candidate Smith has not only funded supply drops for areas affected by the mysterious EMP blasts, but has also enlisted infected to ratify other infected." The television news reporter exclaims directly into the camera, "Let's cut right to the helicopter on the scene."

The station cuts to a camera on board. The initial shot reveals that Smith, in a casual shirt and tie, has earphones on and is holding a microphone.

"Don't worry America; I know you want to survive and that this thing isn't going away with politics. We need hands on, sleeves rolled up, good old fashion, butt-kicking attitude to rid our great country from this mess. Between me, my big friend down there, and your support, we'll get this place cleaned up." Smith puts on a big smile as the camera feed cuts back to the studio.

A familiar German accent speaks up, from the shadowy corner of the helicopters cockpit, "We need to reel in our money maker before he either gets killed or completely eliminates all the dead."

Mike is still on the warpath as the helicopter gets closer and begins to circle the scene. As it lands in the street, a piercing sound is broadcast from loud speakers mounted on the copters belly.

This squeal drives back the remaining dead and leaves Michael standing alone in the street. His battle torn clothes flap in the gust up being created by the choppers propellers as the blood dripping from his soaked hands and mouth is caught up in the strong wind. It's then he recognizes Smith from his posters.

Men in suits are the first to exit the helicopter. They are followed by Smith, who takes a moment to adjust his tie and belt.

"Mr. Eugene, I want to start by saying thank you for throwing your weight, quite literally, behind me and our great cause."

Michael doesn't respond and instead simply breaths deeply.

"You're a big time hero. It's because of you, that I am going to be the next president!"

"I…want…my kids." Mike demands covered in blood.

"Unfortunately sir, they have escaped." Smith tries to say sounding compassionate.

Filled with rage and paranoia, Mike feels he's lying and with his ability to restrain himself no longer inhibited, without a second thought he lunges at Smith.

The guards attempt to protect him, but are both quickly disposed of in a single move. As Smith backs up, the military pilot steps out from the copter with a .45 handgun. As soon as he takes aim, Michael bites through his arm causing him to drop the gun. Then, as he pulls back his bloody appendage, Smith puts his hands up to negotiate.

Smith reminds him, "Your family is still alive and they're out there somewhere. We'll help you find them." He continues, "We knew this was the plan all along. Not you, but this." He says pointing around, "We wanted to destroy the world, so we could take it over. We gave the world Pandora's Box because; we knew they'd open it. Right now, around the world, the virus is spreading like poverty and they all want a piece of the American pie. So, instead of baking their own, they decided to destroy ours. You see, we didn't want a cure; we wanted a disease along the lines of what you see in the mirror these days. When the rest of the world failed, we manipulated them into focusing their attention on 'Plan Z' or the end game. We simply wanted to destroy the foundation of this country using its own citizens against itself until those left would eagerly support the one who rid them of the problem."

From the shadows inside the helicopter, steps out Hans. Again, Michael begins to fill with rage when he sees Hans is still alive.

His thick German accent spills from his pompous lips, "That's where I came in, one head, many arms. You think that train's path was incidental? Or the fact that it and you had to cross the heart of this once fine country? I mean, we were going to use the smart ones we created to clean this all up, but, you proved to be so much more popular." Hans continues, "Your mind is almost stronger than your body, no? I told you using his family against him would work."

"My kids, you said they escaped?"

"He's a politician, he lies for a living. No, you weren't imagining them out there; we were dangling them in front of you like a carrot, so you'd keep working like a good little monster. You did well. Good enough that we haven't had to kill your little girls on live TV, yet."

Mike can't take anymore. The manipulation and arrogance leaves him unable to control himself and he attacks. The injured pilot flips off the siren and what dead are still in the area, quickly begin returning. This gives both Smith and Hans enough time to jump into the copter just as the pilot takes off.

Lunging for his fleeing nemesis, and barely missing, Mike instead grabs the side of the copter just in time.

As they lift higher and higher in the air, a struggle ensues. Mike can see that the pilot's earlier bite is quickly taking affect. Mike is able to reach up and into the cockpit where he's able to tussle enough with Smith to be able to get a grip on his leg. He takes a chunk out of him causing him to scream in pain as he is barely able to hold on.

A sudden twitch of the writhing pilot causes Mike to lose his grip and he falls from the elevated copter hundreds of feet towards the ground.

CHAPTER THIRTY-SEVEN

As if in slow motion, Mike is falling and grabbing for the sky. His mind is racing. Visions of his life flash through his mind. He sees Addison and Al in the yard, Alexis sitting in front of her vanity brushing her hair, and Cindy beside Jason holding the babies.

But it's all interrupted when he eventually lands on a horde of dead with such a thud that it accordions several of them under his weight and knocks him unconscious.

His flashes mangle into a dream state that has him waking up in his own bed. He looks around and for the first time sees that his dream world seems to be complete.

He can hear that the television is on in the other room and without warning his bedroom door bursts open and both of his girls rush in through the door. He instantly begins to tear up and just as they hug, they instead begin to shake him yelling. Their peaceful faces turn to fear until he eventually is awoken to see they are really standing over him.

Apparently in his current state he wasn't killed. Instead, he is able to sit up and hug his girls.

"Dad, you look gruesome." Addy says, "But, I don't care."

He looks up and sees Jason and Sam are almost completely healed.

"You…two…look almost normal?"

"The serum works," Jason answers, "It just takes time to kick in."

Michael leans into his daughter's hugs, letting out a sigh and a heavy breath, "Is this real? Are you all real?"

"Yes." Addy answers.

"Where's…Al?" he asks.

Addy tears up so Alexis answers, "They killed him."

He looks at Addy's devastation and gives her an extra-long hug. It's at this moment they hear the familiar whimper they thought they'd never hear again. It's a sound they haven't heard since before all this happened, since Kingman.

It's Al, not the monster, the half breed mutt and he looks completely normal aside from the bullet hole in his shoulder and blood stains on his fur and around his mouth.

He's limping, but he's alive.

Addy breaks free from her father's arms at the sight, and runs to her friend. As she hugs him carefully, he begins to lick her face. The display puts a smile on everyone's face.

Sam and Jason exchange elbow bumps and congratulatory nods. Alexis hugs her father's neck from behind and Cindy hands the babies to Jason, so she can finally hug her brother.

TO WHOM IT MAY CONCERN:

As the world was told the truth about Candidate Smith and the international conspiracy to use the virus to take control of America, public outrage ensued.

This led to the governments of those involved having heavy sanctions place upon those that denied involvement and a long, hard road to forgiveness for those that admitted their part.

Unfortunately, the geographical damage caused across the heart of the North American continent looks like a slash across the chest of our resilient country. Although, while we did have a way on inoculating both those uninfected and rehabilitating those that have been, the military, minus those found to be in cahoots with the traders, used existing weaponized technology to disperse the solution in the air over the states surrounding the hellish path both I and the runaway airplane took from Nevada to Illinois. Along the coast lines and in other areas unaffected the public health organization began rounds of immunization immediately.

Those that were affected and found wandering were gathered up and placed into a massive camp on the outskirts of our hometown of Kingman, Arizona. Officials sighted it as the perfect remote location to minimize risks.

Their logic astounds me, as it didn't stop anything the first time, but this does allow me to begin closely treating all three varieties while being in an environment that is now more secure.

As far as Smith and Hans, the public was never told of their fate. I know that the virus took hold of the pilot somewhere over Lake Michigan. It took some insisting on my part, but they did drag the lake bottom and recovered all three bodies along with the wreckage.

Luckily, it looks like the impact was so abrupt that the pilot's body was crush by the pressure. Smith was decapitated as the impact sent his body into one of the propellers and Hans was skewered by a section of peeled back metal frame. I guess we'll have to wait to find out if the dead can swim.

This nightmare seems to be approaching its dawn and I am exhausted. I've since stop eating flesh and have upped my dosage of the cure. It will be a while before I am back to normal, but in the meantime, we've survived.

Vegas conglomerates have begun to rebuild, but it will be a long time, if ever, that they regain their tourist capital status as, "What happens in Vegas" definitely didn't stay there. But I guess with enough money anything's possible.

While I do have a positive outlook on the future from here, I am still haunted by the words of the gypsy as she still invades my dreams regularly. Also, I've noticed that while our bodies seem to heal, there is something that remains like a resin in the eyes and minds of those treated. In time, I hope whatever it is fades away like the other physical characteristics. But, for now, I just don't know.

Be strong,

Michael
Recovering dead man

KINGMAN, ARIZONA

As the night falls on the desert, Michael is locking down a gate with the help of several armed guards. His eyes are no longer yellowed and the veins that once spidered throughout his visible flesh have begun to fade.

Addison and Alexis are playing with Rowan and Riot on a makeshift playground that has been assembled for them.

Cindy is asleep, hanging half off a lounge chair; she looks more relaxed than ever before.

Sam is wearing a new uniform and saluting his new commander as he's being issued a rifle.

On the other side of the complex, where the healing dead are housed, the sound of a section of broken chain-link fencing blowing in the wind leads to several footsteps that can be seen heading from the camp and out into the desert hills.

Just over the first hill, the sound of an evil and yet familiar voodoo-like chanting can be heard and it's getting louder.

www.ingramcontent.com/pod-product-compliance
Lightning Source LLC
Chambersburg PA
CBHW060326260626

47160CB00007B/2695